A RELATIVE MATTER
By
Karen Cogan

Karen Cogan

CHECK OUT OTHER BY THIS AUTHOR

http://www.kecogan.blog

Free Contemporary Christian Romance novel Click Here[1]

---

1.   https://us10.list-manage.com/
    subscribe?u=b9804a851b559af817e25e3ba&id=4085af72ba

CHAPTER ONE

. . ⌁ . .

ANNE FOUGHT A TWINGE of anxiety as she scrutinized her grandfather's pinched face. His eyes, pale blue, were sunken and dulled by pain. His hands, once strong, were thin and lined with vivid blue veins. To make matters worse, the summer heat had drained him of energy, leaving him frail and confined to bed.

"Perhaps I should stay home, Grandfather. Indeed you look very ill."

He smiled at her and patted her hand. "You run along, child, and get ready for the assembly. I will have my good Betsy and young Jeremy here to care for me"

He nodded at the upstairs maid and at his grandson, who sat in a chair, absorbed in the study of a colorful atlas.

Anne hesitated. This pale, gaunt, man looked nearly like a stranger. He was nothing of the robust gentleman who had taken her in five years ago, along with her young brother. They had lost their parents to tropical fever in India and been forced to leave the only home they had ever known.

When they had arrived in England, she had not remembered Grandfather; had not seen him since she was a babe in his arms. Yet, he had come in person to meet their ship when she and Jeremy put into port after the long trip. And in their time of grief, he had welcomed them into his home as his kin, the children of his son.

Anne turned to her brother. She smoothed back the dark hair that fell across his forehead and said, "Will you look after Grandfather and make sure he eats something?"

Jeremy nodded. "Certainly. We are going to spend tonight playing our geography game."

Jeremy loved the game Grandfather had invented of taking turns giving the borders of a country and one pertinent fact. The other player had to guess the country. Jeremy liked the game so much, that Anne sometimes wondered if Grandfather would be sorry he had thought of it.

Still, he seemed to enjoy Jeremy's company, brightening each time the boy entered his room. Nonetheless, Anne warned her brother, "No more than a half-hour of the game and then you let Grandfather rest."

She turned to Betsy. "What is there for his supper?"

"There's a nice nourishing soup on the stove. I could bring a bowl up to him, miss."

Anne nodded. "Bring it up at seven o'clock, please. And when he is finished, he must rest."

Betsy curtsied. "Yes, miss."

Anne doubted Grandfather would eat much of the soup. He had little appetite these days. She leaned down and kissed his soft wrinkled cheek.

"I will look in on you before I go," she promised.

He smiled, though his cloudy blue eyes were bereft of their former light. "I will be good as new in a day or two."

"I am sure you will, Grandfather."

They exchanged these words every day, yet every day, he grew weaker.

Not wanting him to see the worry that filled her eyes, she was glad to have him turn his attention to Jeremy, who perched on the bed, eager to begin the game.

She let herself out and tried to recapture her enthusiasm for the assembly as she trod the soft hall rug, past the portraits of ancestors who possessed the same dark hair and blue eyes that marked her line. She paused, staring up at her great-aunt. It gave her an eerie chill to see someone who, at the same age, looked so nearly like herself. Her portrait hung at the end of the hall, having been completed this year on her nineteenth birthday. Would a great-niece stare up at her one day, struck by a likeness of appearance?

She moved along to her room and summoned Polly, her ladies' maid to help her prepare for the assembly. Polly arrived and began the tedious task of arranging Anne's raven curls to fall in ringlets at her temples. It took all of Anne's self-restraint to keep from squirming in her chair as she'd done as a child.

In India, she'd often risen early, before her nanny could come and tend to her. She hated the tiresome ministrations of brushing the tangles from her hair and donning stockings before sitting still to have endless buttons fastened on her shoes. So she had dressed quickly and scampered barefoot out to play before Nanny arrived and before the heavy blanket of heat sapped the energy from all life except the insects that reigned over the land.

The escape had been only temporary because, as soon as she returned, Nanny was waiting; brush in hand to render her fit for the day. She would scold and call her a wild little heathen. Yet her eyes would twinkle when she finished Anne's toilette and she proclaimed her young miss as pretty as a princess. After her appearance was made proper, she was required to sit in during the day and work on her samplers and lessons. Such confinement was difficult for Anne, who longed to walk in the gardens where the flowers scented the air with their exotic fragrance and she chased small quick lizards that she could never catch.

Beyond the high garden walls, the village bustled with life. On a few occasions, she was allowed to accompany one of the servants to market. The sights of the bazaar fascinated Anne. The colorful cloth and jewelry, the choice of fruits and meats, filled her mind with such excitement that she dreamed of them for days. She thought it would be delightful to dash barefoot through the market, laughing and chasing as the native children did. She longed to wander past the tall garden gate and follow her tall handsome father as he went about his military duties, though she never dared do so.

Polly smoothed her hair into submission and asked a question that brought her back to the present. "What do you plan on wearing tonight, miss?"

"You can fetch the blue silk with the cream lace trim."

Polly grinned. "It looks lovely on you, miss, what with your fair complexion."

Anne slid into the dress and Polly fastened the buttons.

Anne was just donning her slippers when Betsy knocked at the door. "Mr. Fletcher is here to call for you, miss."

"Tell him I will be right down."

She pulled her shawl over her arms and hurried to her grandfather's room. She knocked gently and stepped inside.

He lay on his back, breathing so softly that she had to step close to see the rise and fall of his chest. He didn't open his eyes and Anne, loathe to disturb him, tip-toed quietly from his chamber. She shut the door softly and glided down the stairs to where Troy Fletcher awaited her.

Troy gazed up with open admiration. "You look beautiful tonight, Miss Tyler."

"Thank you."

Anne studied Troy. In the two months, he had resided in the inn in town, she had never known him not to be impeccably dressed. Tonight was no exception. He had arrived dressed in a top hat, a black evening coat and matching trousers. His fair hair glistened under the light of the hall chandelier. Though he was not a particularly tall man, he carried himself with such grace that one hardly noticed his height.

Anne took his arm and allowed him to escort her to the waiting carriage.

"Have you found a house that would suit you as a residence?" Anne asked.

He helped her into the carriage and then settled himself beside her.

"Indeed I have not. I have particular tastes and nothing so far has satisfied them...in the way of housing, I mean."

The glance he cast Anne caused her to blush. Changing the subject seemed a wise thing to do as she had not yet decided what she thought of Troy. He was a handsome man, square-built and solid. Yet there was something in his green eyes that sometimes gave her pause, something that reminded her of a cat waiting for a mouse.

"Perhaps, coming from London, your tastes are too exacting to fit our country life."

"No indeed. A life in the country is just what I yearn for. I have a good manager to run my business in London. And now, I intend to settle down, buy a fine pair of hunting dogs, and become a country squire."

"That sounds pleasant indeed, though I should think you might miss the gaiety of London after a while."

"Ah, but that is easily solved. I am determined to marry a local beauty and take her to London every year for the season if she should like to go. What do you think of London, Miss Tyler?"

"I have only been there twice. Grandfather took me and young Jeremy for a month just after Christmas for the last two years. The society was very fine and I attended several assemblies where I had my heart's fill of dancing."

"And did you not long to remain? A month is not very long into the season."

Anne shook her head. "I disliked the feeling of competition, of young ladies vying for the most advantageous matches. Anyway, Grandfather brought us only because he felt obligated to introduce me into society. I knew he was eager to return home. So, a month was quite long enough, you see."

Troy reached to encompass her gloved fingers with his own impeccably white-gloved hand. He turned to her with enthusiasm and said, "I do admire your honesty, Miss Tyler. You are not afraid to call things as you see them, though I cannot see how any of the young ladies could compete with a beauty such as yourself."

He raised her hand to his lips and placed a kiss.

Anne pulled her hand gently from his grasp and folded it into her lap. "Indeed, sir, you pay me too great a compliment."

Before he could protest, she went on quickly, saying, "Pray tell me more about your childhood upbringing. I have told you much about India, but I know little about you."

"You know that I was brought up in the city and that my father was a successful merchant. He dealt in fine cloth and spices. He was a man who valued hard work and discipline. Though I am afraid he doted on me a bit, being his only son, he did manage to pass those values on to me. We dined together every night and he schooled me in the trade."

A wistful look passed over Troy's face. He had told her that his father had died scarcely a year ago and Anne supposed he must miss him a great deal.

"I had a stern tutor who held me to task," Troy said.

Anne laughed as he drew his brows into a forbidding scowl.

"Except for trips to Father's office, I hardly left the house until I was sixteen. It was all study, study, study."

Anne frowned. "I thought you mentioned once of a boarding school?"

Troy flushed a bit. "Oh yes, silly of me to forget. I went to boarding school when I turned twelve. Father wanted me to have every advantage that I might become a good man of business like himself."

"And are you a good man of business?"

Troy gestured to his fine clothes. "I shall let you judge that for yourself."

They arrived in the village, shut tight for the night, dark and sleepy until they pulled to a stop below the assembly room that occupied the space above the millinery. Light poured forth like fairy dust, casting a golden glow upon the new arrivals. Music drifted from the open windows where the assembly had just begun.

The hired driver jumped from the carriage to help Anne from her seat. Her pulse beat with eagerness to join the pleasant crowd of locals who were enjoying themselves to the strain of the orchestra. It had been nearly six months since the assembly at Christmas and Anne had missed the chance to see so many old friends gathered together in one place.

The door beside the shop stood open. Anne smoothed her silk skirt and preceded Troy as they climbed the stairs to the second floor. The long rectangular room seemed awhirl with bright-colored summer dresses. Jewelry sparkled under the light of the chandelier and laughter bubbled forth with such merriment that Anne was immediately caught up in the mood.

She greeted several older matrons who lined the edges of the crowd, clapping to the tune of the music. As Troy followed her through the throng, she saw her friend Mariah awaiting a partner for the next dance. Mariah was a pretty girl, short and plump with golden curls and light blue eyes. She would have had a partner but for the fact that there were more women than men attending the assembly.

Anne hugged her. "Have you been well?"

"Yes. Thank you. And you?"

"We are all fine, save Grandfather. He's been ailing these last few weeks."

"I am sorry to hear it. And Father will be sorry, too. He thinks highly of your grandfather."

Anne smiled. "I shall pass on your regards."

She turned to Troy. "I have been remiss in my introductions, I fear. Mariah, this is Mr. Fletcher. Mr. Fletcher, allow me to introduce my friend and neighbor, Miss Sawyer."

Troy matched Mariah's curtsy with a gallant bow. "I am delighted to meet you, Miss Sawyer."

"And I am delighted to meet you, Mr. Fletcher. Do you live hereabouts?"

"Though I am currently staying at the inn, my wish is to find a suitable residence to rent. My business is in London, but I have grown tired of city life and wish for an escape to the country now and again."

"I should think there would be several possibilities. The Stuart's are quitting their residence to reside in Bath. Have you seen it? It has lovely gardens."

Troy gave her a patient smile. "I have seen it and you are quite correct about the gardens. Unfortunately, the residence was not as large as he had hoped to find."

Mariah raised her brows. "Indeed. Then I fear you may have a difficult time suiting your needs in our little hamlet."

Anne linked her arm with Mariah's and said, "I have warned Mr. Fletcher that we are simple folk. Our houses are not as grand and spectacular as in the most fashionable part of London."

Troy fixed Anne with an assessing gaze. "Ah...but I do not want to be in London. If I must simplify my tastes, then I will do so."

"Perhaps the Miller house," Mariah suggested. "It has small attics, but is quite a lovely house."

Troy looked a bit discomfited. "Indeed. I shall have to look. I must confess, however, that I find it difficult to concentrate on housing while in the company of two such lovely ladies. I find my attention is drawn to the music and I see a waltz has just begun."

Mariah smiled. "Indeed it has. You and Anne must go and dance."

Troy bowed. "If you will excuse us. Again, it has been a pleasure to meet you."

Anne gave Mariah a parting smile before allowing Troy to draw her onto the dance floor. For a squarely built man, he led so smoothly that she felt as though she were floating on air. As they glided past other couples who were happily entranced in one another's arms, Anne decided that the waltz was the most romantic of all dances.

"You dance superbly," Troy complimented as they whirled past a couch filled with watching matrons who fanned themselves with bright oriental fans.

Anne smiled up at him. "It is truly you, Mr. Fletcher, who deserves the compliment, yet I thank you all the same."

Troy cocked a brow at her. "You say you have only been to London twice. Outside of India, have you never been to other cities, other countries?"

"No, I have not. We are quite the homebodies here, I am afraid. And you? Have you traveled widely?"

Troy gave her a bright smile. "Why yes, I have toured the continent, though I never meant to imply anything lacking by your staying at home."

Anne smiled just as brightly. "Have no fear, for I have taken no offense. Only tell me what it was like to cross the sea and visit our neighbors."

"It was magnificent. I saw cities filled with shops and fine galleries. And there was beautiful countryside with snow-topped mountains and blue lakes. And I shall never forget how beautiful it was where I crossed the Seine into Heidelberg. It wound like a long harmless snake through the city."

Anne bit her lip. "Really. I know very little about these things, and yet, I always thought the Seine flowed through Paris."

Troy's fair cheeks turned the shade of twin roses. "Of course. How careless of me. I meant to say Paris. It is easy to get confused when one has seen so much."

"Of course. It was understandable."

Anne thought Mr. Fletcher looked relieved when the dance ended.

"Would you like some refreshment, perhaps some supper?" he asked.

"Only some punch. It is warm in here, do you not think so?"

Troy nodded. "It is warm. I will go directly to fetch punch. Perhaps you would like to have a rest."

Yes. I think I shall sit and visit with Mariah."

Troy took leave on his mission while Anne sought out Mariah. She spotted her leaving a tall handsome partner before seating herself for a rest upon a settee. Anne stared at the retreating gentleman before crossing to join her friend. She settled beside Mariah and said, "Who is that man? I do not believe I have ever seen him."

Mariah giggled. "But of course you have, only it has been a very long time. He is from Westerfield Manor. He has been long away from the estate but now has come back. Old Lord Westerfield's health is failing and he needs his son."

Anne gasped. "That is the young Lord Westerfield? I met him once several years ago when he was home for Christmas. He was a gangly boy with black hair and eyes who reminded me of a crow."

Mariah chuckled. "He has changed a great deal, has he not? And he is such a gentleman. When he saw me sitting alone, he asked me to be his partner."

Anne could not take her eyes off the transformation of the young lord. Time had made him tall and square-shouldered and replaced his slim build with muscle. His former unmanageable locks were now silky raven hair that rested atop his impeccably white cravat.

"So he is home for good?" she asked, without taking her eyes from Lord Westerfield.

"He told me he planned to take up residence and manage his father's estate."

Anne cast a last covert look at the Young Lord Westerfield as Troy returned with the punch. He handed a dainty cut glass cup to each lady "You must be thirsty, too, Miss Sawyer. Please have some punch."

"Thank you, Mr. Fletcher. It was kind of you to think of me."

Anne raised the cup to her lips and tasted the fruity nectar. It was thick and quite sweet, so she sipped it slowly and savored the scent of fresh oranges and pineapples. When they finished, at last, Troy went off to return their cups.

A waltz ended and the orchestra struck up for a reel. Anne saw Mariah's eyes widen. She grabbed Anne by the hand and said, "He is coming this way, Lord Westerfield, I mean."

Anne started to turn about when Mariah whispered tartly, "Do not turn around. He will think we are watching him."

Anne stifled a giggle. "And are we not?"

Mariah squeezed Anne's hand. "Yes, only we do not want him to know."

Lord Westerfield paused beside Anne. He bowed and said, "Miss Sawyer, might I have the additional pleasure of knowing your friend?"

"Indeed. Lord Westerfield, may I present Miss Anne Tyler."

Anne nodded as she looked into Lord Westerfield's intensely dark eyes. Her heart skipped a beat at how handsome he had become. His brows were thick and as ebony as his eyes. His jaw was firm and his nose as straight as a Grecian statue.

"I wondered if Miss Tyler were unengaged, perhaps I might have this dance."

"That would be lovely," she answered. And without a thought to Troy, she tripped off with Lord Westerfield, leaving Mariah to stare after their retreating forms.

If she had thought Troy a good dancer, she was twice as impressed with Lord Westerfield who led her onto the floor and bowed with a vibrancy that was lacking in her previous partner. As they took hands to dance to the end of the row, he said, "I feel I have met you before, yet I cannot place the occasion."

"Yes, it was at least four years ago at a Christmas party at the Stuart residence. I believe you were home for a break from school."

"I remember the party. I fear I was somewhat reclusive. I doubt we even spoke."

"While you did give off the impression of a reserved nature, I would hardly have known what to do if you had spoken to me."

They parted at the end of the lines and clapped while the other partners made their way down the row. When they were reunited once more, Anne asked, "May I make bold as to ask how you like being back in our village?"

Lord Westerfield shook his head. "I did not expect to like it well at all."

He gave her a smile that lit his dark mischievous eyes. "Yet, I find my opinion improving as I make new acquaintances."

"Is that so?"

"Indeed it is. When I left school, I took a tour of the continent. Upon completing the tour, I lived with my uncle in London. He has a prosperous business that I will inherit one day. I had great fun learning about it until I was summoned home."

"I hope you shan't be bored."

"I am sure I shall not."

The sparkle in his dark eyes sent goosebumps along her arms.

The dance ended as did the enchantment of her spell when she saw Mariah speaking with Troy at the edge of the crowd. He sent her a look of disapproval before returning to his conversation.

When they reached them Mariah said, "Mr. Fletcher was kind enough to keep me company while you were engaged."

"Mr. Fletcher is an obliging gentleman, to be sure," Anne replied. "I should like to introduce him to Lord Westerfield."

As the men shook hands, Anne was struck by the contrast between them, one tall and dark, the other a head shorter and quite blond. After they had sized each other up a moment, Troy said, "I do not believe I have seen you before. Have you newly arrived?"

"Yes, only last week. I have come to help my father manage our estate."

"Lord Westerfield has had a tour of the continent. It would be fun to hear each of your opinions," Anne said.

Responding quickly to her remark, Troy said, "That would be of interest to us, but I doubt you ladies would find it amusing. And I am sure that there is a lovely supper laid out. Shall we go in to it?"

He held out his arm to Anne and she had no choice except to take it and leave Lord Westerfield to escort Mariah. Troy leaned to her and said, "May I tell you again how charming you look? I feel it an honor to escort you."

Anne flushed, wishing she could understand why his compliments made her uncomfortable. She forced a bright smile and said, "Why, thank you, Mr. Fletcher. You are kind indeed."

They joined the throng in line at the supper where the ladies filled their plates with ham, beef, small cakes, and biscuits. They stood and chatted as they ate their refreshments. More than once, Anne noticed Lord Westerfield's gaze lingering upon her face.

After they finished their repast, she did not see Lord Westerfield again, except for glimpses across the dance floor. She danced the remaining dances with Troy and other assorted young men who asked for her favor.

They ended the evening by dancing the "Roger de Coverley". By then the hour was late. They retrieved their wraps and settled into the carriage. Anne felt pleasantly drowsy and suspected that the soup had been spiked with negus. In her relaxed state, she was caught quite unaware when Troy reached across to take her hand and impart upon an impassioned confession.

CHAPTER TWO

"IT CANNOT HAVE ESCAPED your attention, Miss Tyler, that I admire you most ardently. Indeed, I think you are the most splendid creature ever put on the earth. I am never happier than when I am in your company."

Anne felt her ease evaporate. Her alarm grew as he leaned toward her, his face inches from her own.

"I do not wish to press you for an answer, yet I beg you to consider this a declaration of my fervent admiration and my desire to marry you. You will never want for anything if you consent to become my wife."

Anne drew back. "Mr. Fletcher, we have known each other only a short time and we know so little about one another. You are correct in assuming that I cannot give you an answer right away."

"I understand. Naturally, you are nervous regarding marriage. Tell me, what can I do to win you over?"

"Give me time, time to think and time to know you better."

He released her hand as he sat back in his seat. "A reasonable request. You may take as long as you like, for I am sure that we are meant to be together and that, in time, you will agree."

Though she could not object to his words, there was an impatient edge to his tone that disturbed her. Was it only that he was a spoiled only son who was used to getting what he wanted? If so, he would find that she cared little about his tempers. She had determined to marry only and if she found a man whom she loved without reserve, a man to whom she could trust her entire heart.

Troy kept to his promise not to press her. They spoke only of the ball and the people who had attended. He asked so many questions about everyone from Mariah to Lord Westerfield that Anne felt exhausted by the time she reached home.

They clattered up the cobbled drive to see the warm glow of twin lanterns beckoning beside the solid oak door. Troy handed her from the carriage and pressed a kiss upon her gloved palm.

"Will you think about what I have said, my dear Miss Tyler?"

"I promise that I shall consider your proposal."

"Then I will take my leave with a heart full of hope and wonderful memories of the evening."

He bowed and released her hand.

Feeling as though she were escaping, she scurried to the door, which Arthur, the butler, held open. He took her wrap. As he shut the door behind her, she heard the sound of the carriage pulling away. She climbed the stairs and retreated to her chamber where Polly helped her prepare for bed. She climbed into the crisp, white, lavender-scented sheets and began to dream.

Just a bit later when the household had settled to sleep, a man, clad in dark trousers and shirt, crept to the rear entrance of the kitchen door, stopped and peered into the darkness. A young serving woman emerged from the shadow of the doorway and hurried to meet him. In whispered tones, she said, "I have been waiting."

"Did anyone see you leave your quarters?"

"Not a soul."

The girl pulled her shawl about her as the man hurried her from the back of the house and across the cobblestone drive. He sent a wary glance at the darkened windows that stared down from the stone-cut Georgian home. It would be a disaster for him if anyone should see him. Yet, he took comfort from the quiet stillness from which no one stirred.

He grasped the girl by the arm and said, "The carriage is just beyond the line of trees. We can take a drive toward the village."

He fairly tossed the girl into the carriage before climbing in beside her. He waited until the driver turned his attention to the horses to whisper, "The old man, how is he?"

The girl grinned. There was just enough moonlight to display her prominent buck teeth. "He is nearly done for, another day at the most, and he will be dead."

"You have done your job well and will get everything you deserve."

The girl wriggled on the seat. "Oh, I shall be happy when we can be together. And I shall have fine things to wear. And perhaps we may have a carriage of our own."

The man tried to hide his distaste for the creature. Eager as he was to dispose of her, he knew he must be patient. He patted her hand and said, "It will not be long now until you get your reward for helping me. And all for seeing that a bit of arsenic found its way into an old man's soup."

They reached a small forest of sorts that lay mid-way from the village. The man instructed the driver to halt. "Could you stop for a bit? It is a lovely night and I fancy a walk among the trees."

The girl hesitated. "We are having a lovely ride."

He took her hand. "But not as romantic as a walk alone through the forest. I fancy having you all to myself."

At that, she giggled and allowed him to help her from the carriage.

The driver lit his pipe and settled himself for a bit of rest. It mattered not to him how long they dallied. He was being paid for the use of his conveyance.

After a bit, the man returned alone and said, "We had a bit of a spat. As she does not wish my company, my companion is determined to walk back."

The driver shrugged as the man settled himself in the carriage. He had paid little attention to either of them. It was no matter to him what they did as long as he was paid.

The next morning, Cook looked about and scowled before asking the scullery maid, "Where is Mary? She is not still abed?"

"I do not know where she is, ma'am. She was gone from her bed when I got up."

"Stupid girl. Go and look for her again. And if you find her, tell her I shall box her ears."

"Yes, ma'am."

The girl returned and reported no sign of Mary.

Cook shook her several voluminous chins and said, "Probably ran off during the night with some bloke from the village. Well, good riddance I say of her, going off with no notice. Divide up her things and forget she was ever here."

"Yes, ma'am."

Instead of forgetting about Mary, Cook spent the morning grumbling about the inconvenience of being short-handed. Poor Lucy, the scullery maid, had to carry her share of the work as well as Mary's and with no thanks from Cook, who was as short-tempered with her as if the whole thing were her fault.

When Betsy returned from taking up the old master's breakfast gruel, she reported that he was very ill indeed. "He ate nothing at all and his color is all wrong. He is blue around the lips and very cold. Miss Anne is sitting with him. She told me not to wake the young master yet."

Cook shook her head. "He is old and frail. We have all seen this coming."

"Nonetheless, he is a good-tempered master and I shall miss him," said Betsy.

Anne spent the morning holding her grandfather's hand and coaxing him to sip at his tea. In the few moments that he awoke, he was possessed of such delirium that he did not seem to recognize her.

Just after noon, when his breathing became very shallow, she rang for Betsy. "Summon Master Jeremy from his studies. I fear the end is very near."

Jeremy came pale-faced into the room. "Is Grandfather going to die?"

Anne pulled him near her on the large cushioned chair. "I am afraid so, dear. He is old and very sick."

Jeremy wiped away tears. "I do not want him to die."

"I know. But Grandfather would wish for us to be brave, and we must do as he would wish."

"I will try, though it is very hard."

Anne put her arm around her brother. "I know, dear. It is hard for me, too."

They sat watch until early afternoon when the elderly gentleman breathed his last. Anne held Jeremy as he lost his valiant struggle not to weep. Anne wiped at her tears as the entire household mourned for the kindly man who had overseen his grandchildren and servants with compassion.

The vicar arrived to speak words of comfort, yet Anne could feel only a cold numbness spreading through her heart. Why must those she loved be taken from her? It did not seem fair. And now Jeremy was all she had left. In her distress, she held on to him so tightly that he squirmed away and knelt beside his grandfather to weep.

"Your grandfather has a nephew over in London, does he not?" the vicar asked.

Anne vaguely remembered that Grandfather had a nephew she had never met. "I believe he does."

"Would you like for me to take care of notifying him?"

"Yes. That would be very kind. Thank you."

They had the burial two days later at two o'clock in the afternoon. A wide assortment of folk gathered in the churchyard to see Mr. Tyler lowered into the ground. Tears flowed freely from men and women, gentry and tenants. Anne wept with the brokenness of heart that she had not endured since the death of her parents. They were alone again, she and Jeremy, and this time they had no loving grandfather waiting to take them in. It frightened her to know that Jeremy's welfare, as well as her own, lay completely in her hands. She was aware that Grandfather's nephew, if still alive, would become the guardian of the estate until Jeremy came of age. It would be years before Jeremy would take control of the manor. In the meantime, Anne could be thrown out to live on the pension Grandfather provided in his will. It was a frightening proposition at best.

At the end of the service, she felt someone place a hand beneath her elbow. She looked up into Lord Westerfield's shockingly dark eyes that were softened by sympathy. He gazed down at her. "On behalf of myself and my father, who could not come today, allow me to express our deepest condolences. Your grandfather was a friend to us for many years."

She wiped her eyes on her lace handkerchief and said, "I thank you for your kind words. Grandfather held you both in high regard."

Lord Westerfield shook his head. "He will be missed by all of us."

"Indeed he will."

"Is there anything that I may do for you?"

"No. The vicar has been very kind to us and Grandfather has a solicitor in the village who will handle his affairs. But thank you for asking."

He bowed. "Please do not hesitate to call on me if there is any way I may assist you."

When he departed, she felt chilled, as though a shadow had moved across the sun, leaving her more bereft than ever. She shivered and wondered at her strange reaction. Young Lord Westerfield had an odd effect on her, though why it was so, she did not know. She knew only that she had never felt so intensely aware of the presence of any other man.

She had little time to dwell on it before the vicar ushered them to the carriage that was waiting to carry them home. Jeremy, who had spoken little for the last two days, asked Anne, "What is to become of us?"

"We will find that out after the vicar notifies Grandfather's nephew. The will states that the property shall pass to 'the heir of his body'. That is you. Yet, I believe his nephew will be your guardian. He will decide whether I may remain in the house. And if I do not, do not worry, Grandfather has provided for me in his will."

She tried to smile and found it so impossible that she gave up and stared at the passing countryside. She remembered how frightened they both had been five years ago when they had first set eyes on this road. They had not known what to expect until they arrived at Grandfather's house and found that it was lovely and that life was pleasant there.

She tore her thoughts away from the past because the past would not count now. If only she knew more about grandfather's nephew, what sort of man he might be, it might ease her mind. But having no such knowledge, all she could do was wait and hope for his indulgence to let her remain at the estate. For she could not bear to think of Jeremy being reared in the care of a stranger.

The next few days saw a steady stream of callers. Though propriety required her to accept these condolences, she found them a strain on her nerves. Worst of all was the afternoon when Mr. Fletcher came to pay his respects.

"I have been away and only just heard about your grandfather. I have come to extend my deepest sympathy. I know you must miss him."

"I do."

"I suppose young master Jeremy will inherit.'

Anne nodded. "Grandfather has a nephew who will become his guardian. I expect to hear from him soon. I hope he will allow me to stay on."

Troy cocked his brow. "And if you do not?"

Anne shrugged. "Grandfather has left me a pension."

"Still, it would be hard for a young woman to set up a house alone. Perhaps the timing is not best to say this, but still, I must. You know it is my ardent desire for us to marry. If you will consent, you will not have to worry about your relative's wishes. I will provide a home for you."

Anne knew she should feel grateful for the offer, yet she could not. If she should choose to wed, she wanted it to be a joyous occasion. Now, mourning Grandfather as she did, could not summon the faintest interest in marriage.

"I am sorry, Mr. Fletcher. You are kind to offer, but I am still too heart-sore to make a decision."

"Then I shall give you more time. But I do urge you to consider my proposal. I would hate to see you cast alone into society."

Anne felt a bit annoyed by his persistence. "Do you not think it better to be alone than to make the wrong decision regarding marriage?"

A brief flash of impatience showed on his face before he composed himself to say, "Of course. Yet I am convinced that we would not be making the wrong decision."

Anne had tired of the conversation. The high collar on her black mourning dress was hot and itchy. She longed to go to her room, slip out of the dress and crawl under her cool sheets. But first, she must get rid of her guest.

"Your confidence does you justice. When, and if, I share your assurance, I shall give you my answer," she promised.

She stirred, planning to rise and put an end to the interview.

He stood and grasped her by the arms, pulling her up to face him.

"In all the time I have escorted you about the village, I have found no fault with you. I hope you will form a similar opinion of me. I shall leave you now with these words."

He pulled her so close that her unease turned to alarm.

"You are dear to me, my darling Miss Tyler, so very dear. If you should need me, just send word to the inn."

She struggled a bit to pull free, fearing he would try to kiss her.

"Please, you are hurting my arms."

"I am sorry."

He released her and she stepped away.

"Good day, Mr. Fletcher. And thank you for calling."

After he bid her good-bye, Arthur handed him his hat at the door. Anne sighed with relief when she heard it click closed behind him. She mounted the stairs and stopped at Jeremy's room. She found him on the floor, pouring despondently over his atlas. Kneeling beside him, she said, "You miss Grandfather and the games you played together."

Jeremy nodded. "He was my best friend."

Anne put her arm around Jeremy's shoulders. "Mine, too, dear. We shall have to give ourselves time to get over our loss."

"What is going to happen to us?"

"I do not know, yet. But as long as we are together, we will be fine."

Jeremy smiled bravely up at her. "You are my best friend now, Anne."

She squeezed him gently. "And you are mine."

She went to her room and fell gratefully into bed for an afternoon rest. Before she fell asleep, she thought over Troy's visit. Though he had been quite solicitous in saying she need only send a message to him if she needed him, she had not felt inclined to accept his offer.

Who else had offered her help? She thought back to the funeral. It was the handsome Lord Westerfield with his pirate-black eyes. Why did she find his invitation so inviting when she had not felt the same about Mr. Fletcher. It was not because Lord Westerfield would inherit an estate. She cared little for social position.

No, it was the disposition of each man. Lord Westerfield intrigued her while Troy made her uneasy. This realization led her to the conclusion that she could not accept this proposal from Troy only because it came at a needful time in her life.

She could not marry him unless she were to be convinced beyond a shadow of a doubt that their love would be deep and enduring, the kind of love her parents shared before their death from tropical fever.

She fell asleep with these doubts plaguing her mind and with the dark eyes of a pirate haunting her dreams.

She awoke to see the long shadows of late afternoon creeping across the red roses that bloomed in her plush rug. She tossed back the white coverlet on her bed and crossed the room to peer out of her window into the back gardens of the house. The gardener was whistling as he trimmed the hedges, the kitchen girl was collecting herbs for supper stew from the small square garden.

Everything was returning to normal. Soon the household would have a new member. Eventually, Grandfather's memory would fade. But not from Anne and not from Jeremy. Of this, she was sure.

The next morning Anne awoke unable to stand the thought of another day closeted morosely in the house. She donned her black silk mourning gown and went down for a light breakfast, after which she told Arthur, "Tell John Coachman to have the carriage brought round. I wish to visit Miss Sawyer."

"Yes, Miss."

She finished her toiletry and donned her hat and gloves.

She left Jeremy in the charge of his tutor, Mr. Ames. Then, in the glorious sunshine of a summer morning, she found the carriage awaiting her departure. The young man who drove her was new, having been just hired by the 'ostler and she was obliged to give him directions to Mariah's house.

When they arrived, he helped her down and settled on his seat to wait.

Anne wound her way past the flowers that lined the drive and presented herself at the door. She was well-known to the staff and was immediately invited to the parlor to await Miss Sawyer.

After a few moments, Mariah came down. She greeted Anne with an enthusiastic smile. "What impeccable timing you have. I have just dressed and was ready to come down. Will you not have tea with me?"

"I would love tea."

Mariah ordered tea and cakes. While they waited, Mariah asked, "How have you been? I planned to call on you this week and see how you have fared since the funeral."

"I must admit to lowness of spirit. Jeremy and I have grown very close to Grandfather in the last five years. We will miss him sorely."

"What is to happen to you and Jeremy?"

"I do not know. Grandfather has a nephew that is named guardian until Jeremy comes of age. Perhaps he will let me stay on at the estate."

"Oh, he must. I could not bear to have you go away. And where would you go?"

"I would live on the funds that Grandfather left me. Perhaps I could take a small house and live frugally with a servant or two."

Mariah stomped her small foot. "That must not happen. I shall speak to your Grandfather's nephew on your behalf if he proves ungenerous."

Anne laughed at her friend, "And what will you say?"

Mariah looked perplexed. "I do not know exactly. I will appeal to his best instincts."

She brightened and added, "Perhaps I shall marry him and become the mistress of your estate. Then, I should persuade him to let you stay on."

"I am sure he is quite old, fifty at least."

"La, I did not think of that. Then I shall not marry him."

She grinned mischievously, "Unless of course, I fall in love."

She studied Anne. "And what of you? You have been privileged to the steady attention of Mr. Fletcher for the last two months. You should have seen him when you were dancing with Lord Westerfield. He was quite beside himself with envy."

"Was he? I did not notice."

"It is no wonder. You did not notice because you were dancing with Lord Westerfield. Is he not the most handsome of men? Of course, Mr. Fletcher is handsome, too."

"That he is. And yet, there is something about him that gives me pause. There is a disturbing inconsistency of manner and in the things he says."

"La, you worry too much. He seems a perfectly charming gentleman to me."

"Perhaps you are right. Still, he has been pressing me for an answer to his proposal of matrimony. He offered to provide a home for me. And yet, I do not know that I love him."

"Is that so important?"

"It is to me."

Their tray arrived and Mariah occupied herself with a small cake to go along with her tea. She seemed to be deep in thought until at last, she said, "I am not so sure that love is necessary for a successful marriage. I believe that I could be quite satisfied with many a handsome man who possessed a pleasant disposition."

Anne's silken brow wrinkled into a frown. "I do not feel the same. I want a man who cares only for me and I for him. I could only look forward to marriage if it was preceded by the deepest romantic affection."

Mariah shook her head. "I wish you luck in finding such a romance. For my part, I am not sure that it exists."

"If it does not, I shall not marry at all."

Anne took a bite of teacake and made up her mind that, without a change of heart, marriage to Mr. Fletcher was out of the question.

She remembered her alarm when she thought he might kiss her. Would she not have welcomed his kiss if she were truly in love? But then, how could she know since she had never been in love.

She puzzled over the matter as they finished tea.

At last, Mariah suggested a walk in the garden. Anne agreed quickly, hoping the fresh air might clear her mind. She followed Mariah to the French doors which opened out to a row of rose bushes in full bloom. Next to the house, hollyhocks grew on tall stalks, presenting their frilled flowers to the sun. Sweet William, sweet peas and asters bloomed along the ground, scenting the air with a myriad of fragrances.

The sun was warm, baking down upon Anne's black-clad shoulders. Yet, despite the heat, it was a fine day to be outdoors. They walked along a hedge and watched a brown sparrow hopping along the top branches. A rabbit ran across their path, anxious to reach the safety of his burrow.

They stopped to watch the few puffy clouds playing about the sky. A friendly breeze caressed Anne's hair, reminding her of the warm breezes of her childhood. And she was grateful for the reminder. In India, she and Jeremy had carried on after the death of their parents. They would carry on again. She must not feel sorry for herself for losing either her parents or Grandfather. She must think of what was best for herself and Jeremy.

Mariah interrupted her thoughts to say, "I forgot to tell you that Mr. Fletcher paid me a compliment the night of the assembly."

"What did he say?"

Mariah's blond curls danced as she said, "He said that I looked very lovely in my dress. I hope it does not bother you that he spoke to me so. For the most part, he scanned the dance floor, watching for you."

"It does not bother me."

Anne wondered that it did not. If she were truly in love with Mr. Fletcher, would she mind that he had admired Mariah?

After they had walked a bit longer, she took her leave, still pondering her feelings. As her carriage clattered along the rutted road, she tried to imagine what Grandfather would advise her to do. Would he tell her that the romantic feelings she desired would come in time if she married Mr. Fletcher? But what if they did not?

With these unsettling thoughts in mind, her carriage rounded the drive giving Anne a clear view of another carriage parked near the entry. She could only think that it was Mr. Fletcher come for her answer. And what would she say?

CHAPTER THREE

..⚓..

ANNE SET HER JAW WITH determination as she entered the house. She would not be pressed into a marriage, no matter how persuasive Mr. Fletcher might be. She had not the proper feelings to enter into matrimony and doubted that closer association was going to produce them. Yet, she would be willing to consider him if he would only be patient with her and allow her to be sure,

She handed her bonnet and shawl to Arthur as he announced her guest. "A gentleman, Lord Westerfield, to see you, miss."

Anne felt her heart skip a beat. All of her mental preparation had been directed toward facing Mr. Fletcher. She felt unprepared to greet the dark-eyed man had had the strange effect of making her feel both flustered and exhilarated at the same time.

Anne smoothed her skirts and took a deep breath. She bit her lips to redden them and then stepped into the parlor. She found Lord Westerfield seated upon the rose-patterned satin sofa. He stood when she entered, his entire countenance lifting at the sight of her.

She smiled and said, "Lord Westerfield, how kind of you to call."

"I could not help myself. I hope you will not be offended if I say that you look lovely, even in mourning."

"I am not the least offended. Please, do sit down."

He took a seat on the sofa while Anne settled onto the straight-backed satin-seated chair. Feeling a bit awkward, she began to prattle, "I have just been to see my friend, Mariah Sawyer. You must remember her from the assembly. She lives not far from here at

Meadowdown. They have a lovely garden and we went walking. It often raises my spirits to be out of doors."

She paused to take a breath and decided she could not keep running on. She decided to ask, "How did you like the assembly? Did you have a good time?"

"I did indeed."

He watched the becoming flush that still colored her cheeks. He did not know when he had ever seen a more charming creature, devoid of the cunning and flirtatious airs that he despised in a female.

He smiled at her and added, "I enjoyed the dancing in particular, especially when a certain young lady was my partner."

As Anne thought back about the dance, she felt a stab of disappointment. He had danced only a little with her and several dances with Mariah. Surely, the purpose of his visit was to learn more about Mariah. Perhaps he wanted to know if she had a steady suitor.

She hoped her feelings did not show on her face as she said, "I am happy that you had a good time. I suppose you wish to know if the young lady is spoken for. Let me relieve your mind and tell you that she is not and would welcome a call, I am sure."

He beamed. "That is a great relief. When I saw the blond young man, I assumed there might be a special attachment."

"No indeed. They are only casually acquainted."

"That is a relief."

"I am glad to put your fears at rest."

"Then I may call again?"

"Have you been already?"

Lord Westerfield looked perplexed. "Why yes. Your state of grief has led you to forget. That is understandable."

"I am surprised Mariah did not mention it."

"Why should Mariah mention it?"

Anne flushed, embarrassed to be caught prying when the courting affairs of others were none of her concern. "Indeed, why? Anyway, I am sure she will be most happy to receive you."

Lord Westerfield's coal-black brows pulled together in puzzlement. "Why should she receive me?"

"You asked me if it would be proper to call upon her."

Now Anne felt as thoroughly confused as Lord Westerfield looked.

"I do not wish to call upon Mariah. I wish to call upon you. Is there any reason why I may not do so?"

For a stunned moment, Anne stared at him. Then a blush crept across her cheeks.

"Oh, I have misunderstood."

His frown eased as he noted her discomfort. "I thought as much. Perhaps I was not clear."

"No. It was my mistake. Please forgive me. I did not mean to be coy."

He smiled as he said, "I should not like you so much as I do if I thought that you had. Now, pray do not keep me in suspense. May I continue to call upon you?"

Even though she had never felt more flustered, Anne began to laugh. "Of course you may call upon me. I shall look forward to it."

Lord Westerfield laughed, too. "I see that I shall enjoy making your acquaintance. You are like a breath of fresh air. And since you are so fond of the outdoors, perhaps the next time I call, we might take a stroll in your park. The weather has been uncommonly fine."

"It has indeed. We shall have to hope that it lasts. If it is raining, we shall have tea indoors."

He smiled at Anne. "A perfect solution."

He wondered if she had any idea how appealing she looked, perched like a graceful bird upon the chair, her dark hair glimmering and her blue eyes shining. He would have been content to stay and study her lovely face. Yet he knew Father was expecting him to return and go over their accounts.

He slapped his thigh. "I must go. Yet, I cannot leave without inquiring how you and your brother are withstanding the loss of your grandfather. Are you feeling any more cheered?"

She wanted to reply that his company had done wonders for her spirits. Instead, she said, "The wound is not so fresh anymore. However, I think Jeremy feels it most keenly. He and Grandfather were great friends. They spent a lot of time playing games together, especially once Grandfather was confined to bed."

"Perhaps you and Jeremy would like to come out and see our new litter of pups. They will become fine hunting dogs one day."

"What a wonderful idea. I am sure it would cheer him."

"Then you may tell him that I shall call upon you both and transport you to Westerfield. Would tomorrow afternoon be convenient?"

"It would be lovely."

"Then I shall call at three o'clock."

"I shall tell Jeremy."

Lord Westerfield rose.

"I shall bid you good-day until tomorrow."

He bowed gracefully, a lock of black hair falling boyishly across his forehead. Anne curtsied, admiring both the man and his straightforward manner.

When Arthur had fetched Lord Westerfield's hat and bid him good-day, Anne went up to find Jeremy, sure that he would be thrilled by the opportunity to see the puppies.

Not to her surprise, Jeremy came more alive than she had seen him in days. The prospect of playing with the pups filled him with excitement. "Do you suppose we could buy one? I have wanted a dog ever so long."

Anne started to say they would ask Grandfather and then closed her lips tightly. She blinked back sudden tears that pricked at her lids. When she felt more composed, she looked into his small hopeful face and said, "We will see, dear. I do not know that Lord Westerfield wishes to sell them."

If he did indeed plan to sell some of the puppies, she would have to stall Jeremy for time. Since she did not want to prejudice him against his new guardian, she did not tell him the gentleman might have an opinion about the matter. If the puppies were for sale, they would cross that bridge when they came to it.

.. ⌦ ..

LORD WESTERFIELD ARRIVED the next afternoon promptly at three o'clock. He brought a fine barouche carriage that impressed Anne, but not Jeremy. He had thoughts only for the puppies.

"How many are there?" he asked.

Lord Westerfield helped Anne into the carriage and set Jeremy beside her.

"There are six fine healthy pups."

"What do they look like?"

Lord Westerfield climbed into the opposite seat. "You shall find that out when you see them."

"Hunting dogs?" Jeremy asked.

"Indeed. They will be fine hunters someday."

Anne tapped Jeremy's knee. "Stop asking Lord Westerfield so many questions. You will tire him out before we ever get there."

Lord Westerfield winked at Jeremy. "We men have a keen interest in our animals that women do not understand. Is that not right, Jeremy?"

Jeremy nodded, pleased to be called a man at the tender age of nine years old. He liked Lord Westerfield with his friendly black eyes and ready smile. He liked him much better than that stuffy Mr. Fletcher who had been hanging around Anne. He could not imagine Mr. Fletcher inviting him to see puppies.

Anne turned to Lord Westerfield and said, "How is your father today?"

"In fine spirits. He is looking forward to seeing you both. I believe he needs a bit of stirring up now and again as he does not get about much these days."

"I shall be glad to see him also. It is lovely to have such kind neighbors. It makes sorrows easier to bear."

Lord Westerfield looked deeply into her blue eyes and said, "I would think myself blessed indeed if I might ease even a mite of your sorrows."

Looking into his kind eyes, Anne knew that he meant every word. His honesty impressed her and she realized that she coveted Lord Westerfield's good opinion as she did very few people. He was unlike the men who were happy to pay her glib flattery that she could easily do without.

Lord Westerfield asked her about her childhood in India and Anne was happy to reminisce until they reached his manor. She sucked in a breath when they reached sight of it. It was an impressive estate. The rolling green grounds swept up to a tall Georgian house with at least a dozen windows showing from ground to attic. The albacore colored stone glistened in the sun, welcoming the guests.

They pulled into the circular drive and alit in front of the broad oak door adorned with a polished brass knocker. Twin cedars stood each side of the door. They were as perfectly trimmed into points as were the bushes that lined the drive.

They entered the great hall and were greeted by a butler in a starched white shirt. "The master is in the drawing-room, sir. He bids you bring in the guests."

They trod the plush red paisley carpet to a sunlit room just off the hall. Inside, a thin, white-haired gentleman sat bundled beside a sunny window. He smiled broadly at the sight of them.

"My dear Miss Tyler and Master Tyler. Forgive me for not rising. It seems my legs have lately grown unsteady."

Anne curtsied. "My lord, it is a pleasure to see you. Though I know you had not visited each other in quite some time, Grandfather always considered you a great friend."

"As I did him. My son tells me you have missed him a great deal."

"I have, sir. He took my brother and me into his home five years ago after our parents died. He was very kind and we loved him a great deal."

"You were both a blessing to him, too. He was lonely before you came, just as I was lonely before my son returned."

He turned a warm smile toward his son that assured Anne that the young lord was a kind son as well as a kind friend. He had willingly returned at the request of his father, given up the excitement of London and cheerfully embraced the running of the estate.

"Would you care for tea?" asked the elder lord.

Anne was on the verge of agreeing when Jeremy began to pull on her sleeve.

"The puppies. Please, Anne, the puppies."

Young Lord Westerfield overheard and said, "I have promised Jeremy that he would see the new puppies. Perhaps Miss Tyler and I might escort him and then come back for tea while he enjoys a romp with them."

He turned to the boy. "Do you mind missing tea?"

"Oh, no sir, not if I can stay with the puppies."

The elder lord laughed. "By all means take the boy to the puppies. Come back when you are ready and I will wait tea."

They left the elder lord still smiling over Jeremy's enthusiasm. However, when Anne got him out to the hall, she began to chastise him. "You must not be cheeky. It was not polite to interrupt like that. I am glad Lord Westerfield's father was not offended."

Jeremy failed miserably at trying to look contrite. "I am sorry."

He turned to Lord Westerfield. "May I really stay with the puppies?"

Lord Westerfield laughed. "Yes, you may."

Anne sighed. She was going to have her hands full with her impetuous young brother. Yet she dared not be too hard on him when he had lost so much. Perhaps he needed understanding more than a firm hand. She hoped so because she could not bring herself to chastise him too harshly.

They followed a quaint cobblestone path from the back of the house, past hedgerows of blooming roses and continued along a cobbled footpath until they entered the stable. It smelled of hay and feed and the musky smell of horseflesh. Several white chickens and a cocky Bantam rooster dodged around their feet, scampering past and serenading them with a cacophony of noisy squawks.

They followed Lord Westerfield to a stall in a far corner of the stable. He opened the door and they walked inside, latching the door carefully behind them.

"We cannot have these little fellows getting under the horses' feet."

Six of the cutest blond puppies Anne had ever seen lay either piled asleep in the corner or scrambling about the stall. They were pudgy and clumsy, tripping over their paws as they scurried to greet their guests.

Jeremy squatted down to pet them as they scrambled into his lap. He laughed as he tumbled over in a heap of puppies. "You must pat them, Anne. They are so very soft."

"I shall make it easy," said Lord Westerfield. He scooped up a chubby puppy and held it so that Anne might see.

She could not help but smile at the charming creature. "Oh, but you are cute."

She reached out and petted the puppy's head. His ears were long and silky, his fur short and soft."

His little tongue found her wrist and he began to bestow his affection.

"I believe he likes you," said Lord Westerfield.

"The feeling is mutual."

Anne wondered who could not like such an adorable creature. He had round black eyes and a short black nose with tiny whiskers. His paws were too big and his tail too short. He smelled of milk and hay and he had tiny sharp teeth.

The mother stirred to her feet. She was a handsome dog, white and shaggy with large black spots. Lord Westerfield set the puppy down and squatted to pet the mother.

"Sadie, old girl, are you feeling forgotten?"

He rubbed her ears and her tail began to wag. He looked up at Anne and said, "She is a fine dog, good-tempered and obedient. Her pups will be good, too."

Jeremy laughed as a pup licked his face. "I should like one ever so much. Will they be for sale? Anne said that I might have one."

Anne blushed as she corrected him. "I did not say that you might have one. I said we would see if it was possible."

"It is quite possible, I assure you," said their host. "I would be happy to save a pup for you. Which one do you fancy?"

"I like the one you were holding."

"You have made a good choice. He is a dandy little fellow. They are still too young to be away from their mother. When he is old enough you may take him. Perhaps I might help you train him to hunt."

Jeremy looked up to Lord Westerfield. His eyes were shining. "I would like that ever so much."

"You are sure you would like to stay and play with them while we go to tea?" Lord Westerfield teased.

Jeremy nodded. "Yes, I would much rather. Thank you."

Lord Westerfield nudged an escaping puppy back inside as he and Anne slipped out the door. He knew his father would be eager for their company. When he had told him about Anne, the older man had been ecstatic. He had spent the last few years hoping that his son would find a girl to suit his fancy. He hoped for grandchildren before his health robbed him of the enjoyment of them. And though it was too soon to know if they would become attached, the young lord knew that it gave his father hope.

He gave Anne an anxious glance as he took her elbow to walk back toward the house. She had been very quiet and held her lip captured between her teeth. Could he have said something wrong? Before he could inquire, she said, "It was kind of you to offer Jeremy his pick of puppies. However, he must understand that, should Grandfather's nephew disapprove, it might be inconvenient for me to take along a puppy if I am forced to move."

He stopped her and looked down into her face. Her dark lashes framed her eyes, eyes that were the deep blue of the sky on a stormy day. Her lips were cherry red, her skin as smooth as a porcelain doll. He longed to run a finger along her cheek, taste her lips and touch her hair. Yet, he knew he dare not do any of these things. Not yet, at least, he told himself.

Even so, for a long moment, they stood staring at one another as though neither could remember the topic of their conversation. Then Anne said, "Do not misunderstand me. I appreciate your generosity in offering Jeremy his pick of puppies."

Lord Westerfield forced his errant thoughts back to the matter at hand. "Do not let that worry you. I should be glad to keep the puppy, even to begin training him if necessary, until you can either take him or decide to leave him with me. He is quite one of my favorites."

"Then you must keep him for yourself."

"I already have a pair picked out for me. The others are going to good homes. It would not be hard to find a home for Jeremy's pup should you not be able to take him."

She smiled and the distress left her eyes. "Then we are both most grateful to you."

"It is I who is grateful to you for your company on this fine day. And for humoring my father by taking tea."

Anne looked surprised. "Oh, but I am very happy to do so."

Lord Westerfield chuckled. "And he is very happy to have you as a guest."

They entered the drawing-room and the elder lord took great pleasure in ordering their tea. And when it arrived, he fussed over Anne until she felt quite self-conscious.

"Take a tart, my dear; they are quite tasty, as are the little cakes. Are you in need of more tea?"

"Thank you, sir, but I have not finished this cup yet."

Anne could neither eat nor drink fast enough to stay ahead of his offer of more food. Still, she found him charming and engaging, especially when his conversation drifted to tales of the younger lord's youth.

"He has always been a good boy, quite too serious as a child, but he has grown out of that, have you not?"

He smiled at his son.

Lord Westerfield nodded. His dark eyes twinkled. "Now I am not serious at all. I live for nothing except a good time."

The elder lord frowned. "You are saying that just to goad me. And you will give our guest quite the wrong impression."

"I am sorry, Father. I am an awful tease. I will trust Miss Tyler to understand that there are a great many things that I take quite seriously."

Anne nodded and assured the elder Lord Westerfield, "Indeed, sir, I believe your son to be quite capable of a serious bent should the need arise."

"Good." The old man beamed. "Then we should all finish our tea. Will you not have another cake, Miss Tyler?"

When Anne had drunk and eaten all that she was capable of holding, they bid the old man good-day and went to collect Jeremy. He loathed to leave the puppies, but when Lord Westerfield invited him to come again soon, they were able to pry him away.

After prattling on for awhile about names for the puppy, Jeremy fell asleep during the carriage ride home. Anne sat across from Lord Westerfield and stole covert glances at his handsome face. Why he intrigued her so completely, she could not tell. She knew only that he did.

After a while, she said, "I do not remember ever hearing about your mother. Has she been gone for a long time?"

"She died when I was but two. I do not remember her. I wish that I did."

"But perhaps you are lucky that you do not remember if you were destined to lose her. I remember my mother and I think it is harder to lose someone you have known and loved than someone you have never known."

"Perhaps you are right. But now we are onto a subject that I fear will make us both sad. So I shall make so bold as to change it and say that I had a wonderful time having tea with you."

"As did I. I hope that you shall come for a walk in our gardens soon. If it is a nice day, we can have our tea outdoors."

He studied her tenderly. "I believe that summer was made just for you. I do not believe I have ever met a lady who takes such pleasure from being out of doors.

She smiled. "Remember that I was reared in India. I am used to enjoying long walks in beautiful gardens. I love it here in England and I would not wish to leave our home. Yet, there are things that I miss."

He leaned forward. She caught her breath at the look in his eyes. It was tender, yet there was something more, a longing that made her heart skip a beat. He gazed at her and said, "You have had hard adjustments in the past. I hope you have only pleasant ones in the future."

His concern for her welfare touched her to the core. She smiled at him and said, "My friends are a great comfort to me now."

"I hope I can be numbered among them."

"Most certainly, sir. You have already proven yourself, my friend."

"Then I am happy, indeed."

They rode in companionable silence until they reached Anne's home. When the carriage stopped, Jeremy sat up and rubbed his eyes. For a moment, he looked confused. Then he said, "I must have fallen asleep."

"I imagine the puppies gave you quite a go," Lord Westerfield replied.

He helped Anne from the carriage and then lifted the still groggy Jeremy to the ground. He left them at the door with a promise to return in a few days for a walk in the garden.

As the carriage clattered away, Jeremy said, "You should marry him, Anne. He is much nicer than Mr. Fletcher."

"Hush, now. We barely know each other. You had better not say anything like that to Lord Westerfield."

"All right. But I like him."

Anne smiled down at her brother. "I like him, too."

The next day a letter arrived by post. Arthur presented it to Anne as she took a late breakfast. She stared at her name, written in an unfamiliar scrawl across the envelope.

"I wonder who has written to me."

She took the letter opener from the salver and sliced the envelope. Inside on a thin sheet of parchment, was a short handwritten note. She scanned to the bottom of the letter and frowned. Who was Bertram Tyler? A glance back at the opening sentence answered her question. Bertram Tyler was Grandfather's nephew.

CHAPTER FOUR

.. ✿ ..

ANNE READ THE LETTER carefully twice through. Bertram Tyler planned an immediate removal from London. He was to arrive within the next two days to reside at Grandfather's house. He gave no details as to who he might be bringing with him or if Anne was invited to remain.

She frowned. Two more days. That certainly gave him little time to have seen to the disposal or packing of his property in London. Perhaps he was leaving that in the hands of a trusted servant.

She set the letter aside with a sigh as there seemed nothing more to be gleaned from the few sparse lines. She mulled it over as she finished breakfast. Then, seized by the desire to discuss it with a friend she decided to dress for an outing and take the letter to Mariah.

She ordered the carriage and had Polly help her into her mint-green cotton day dress with a shiny silk ribbon that tied just under the bust. They arranged her dark hair to be clasped at each side of her head, leaving curls to cascade from her temples. Then she chose a bonnet with green ribands that matched the dress.

She had pulled on her gloves and was preparing to depart when she saw a carriage appear from the line of trees. She squinted, trying to recognize the occupant. Her heart beat quickly with the hope that it might be Lord Westerfield. If so, she would abandon her plan to visit Mariah in favor of sharing the letter with him.

The carriage pulled to a stop and Troy stepped out. He gave her a bright smile and tipped his hat. His flaxen hair shone in the sunlight.

With a glance at her carriage, he said, "I seem to have arrived just as you are planning an outing."

"Yes. I have had a letter from Grandfather's nephew. I was on my way to show it to Miss Sawyer."

Troy raised a brow. His green eyes lit with interest.

"Grandfather's nephew plans to arrive within the next two days," she explained.

She glanced up to see her new carriage driver staring at them with interest. She gave him a disapproving frown and said, "Perhaps you would like to accompany me to visit Miss Sawyer. We could discuss the letter along the way."

"I would be delighted to come along and offer any insight I might have regarding the note."

"That, I would appreciate."

She allowed him to help her into the carriage and they set off to visit Mariah.

She unfolded the note and handed it to Troy.

She watched as he read it carefully.

When he had folded it back again, he said, "It sounds as though he has not made up his mind as to what to do when he arrives."

"I know. But it worries me that it relays so little. Is he bringing a family? And how could he dispose of his things so quickly and come here to reside?"

"Perhaps he has nothing of value of which to dispose of. He may have inherited very little or spent what small amount he had."

"I suppose you could be right. I never thought of that."

"Your grandfather was a first son and so was your father. They inherited land. Perhaps this nephew was a second son. Not everyone is privileged to inherit property."

His voice held a veiled note of bitterness that surprised her. After all, he was the only son of a wealthy man. Perhaps he simply thought the system unfair.

"Yes. It is true," she said, thoughtfully. "Yet, even though Jeremy will inherit, I may be turned out of our home for a time."

"How old is this nephew?"

"I do not know. I have never met him."

"Cheer up, then. Perhaps he is old and will not live long."

Anne stared at him in consternation. "Whatever my circumstances may become, I do not wish him ill."

He took her small gloved hand in his own. "Of course you do not. You are far too kind for that."

The smile he gave her did not reach his eyes. She could not imagine what reason he could have for such odd behavior. And yet, he was right about one thing. If Grandfather's nephew was old, she would not be out of their home for long. And no matter what, Jeremy would inherit one day and things would be put right again.

They got to Mariah's house and were admitted into the parlor while the butler sent a maid to announce their arrival. They did not wait long until Mariah swept into the room, wearing a dark pink dress with puffed sleeves. Her light curls framed her small oval face. Her eyes lit with pleasure when she saw that Troy had accompanied Mariah.

She beamed at them and said, "This is a pleasure. Please sit down and tell me why you are here."

"Indeed we shall."

Anne dug into her pocket and produced the letter.

"Grandfather's nephew has written to me. He plans to arrive here within the next two days. Would you please read the letter and tell me what you think of it?"

"I shall be glad to read it. I am quite curious."

Anne handed the letter to Mariah. Her sable brows puckered as she carefully read every line. After she finished she said, "I do not think it is a good letter at all. He does not say who is coming with him or what he is bringing. How shall you plan for his arrival?"

Anne nodded. "That is exactly what I thought."

Troy stretched his legs languidly. Seeming less concerned by the matter than the ladies, he said, "Why should you go to the trouble to prepare for him? He does not tell you when he is arriving or who he is bringing. I say let him come and make the best of things as they are."

Mariah giggled. "I say, Mr. Fletcher, that is a wicked suggestion."

"It may be a practical suggestion. What else can I do?" Anne asked.

"Exactly," said Troy. "There is nothing else to be done. Anne is not his servant, even if he does have guardianship."

Mariah leaned toward Troy. "That is true. And yet, Anne does not want to give offense to a man who can either turn her out or allow her to stay."

"He will not turn Anne out."

Mariah's eyebrows puckered. "How can you be so sure?"

"When he sees Anne, he will not want to turn her out."

Mariah stiffened perceptibly. "Yes, I am sure you are right."

"Well, I am not at all sure," said Anne. "I am beginning to wish the whole thing was over so that I might know what is to become of us. Anything would be better than remaining in suspense."

Mariah sat back and pretended to study her nails. "Surely you are not worried about your future, Anne. You are a lucky woman. With your beauty, you must have any number of eligible men begging for your hand."

Anne was surprised by the peevish tone of her friend's voice. Whatever had come over Mariah? She sounded as though she was jealous, though Anne could not fathom the reason. She saw nothing in her present circumstance to cause anyone jealousy.

"I will rent a small place in the village if I am forced from my home," she replied coolly.

Troy sat up. His green eyes were dark with disapproval. "Surely you do not mean to live there alone. That is much too scandalous even for a woman as independent as you."

"Grandfather has provided enough pensions for a small staff of servants. I assure you that I do not intend to do anything so improper as to ruin my reputation."

Troy maintained a stern frown while Mariah seemed to cheer visibly.

"Would anyone like tea?" she asked.

"No. Thank you. I cannot stay any longer," Mariah said. "There is much to be done at home. The servants grow lax when I am not there. I had to chastise the downstairs maid yesterday for a layer of dust on the mantel. And Jeremy mopes about with no one to cheer him. He spent such a great amount of time with Grandfather that he misses him dreadfully."

"Then, of course, we must be off," said Troy.

He rose and offered his hand to Anne. As he assisted her to her feet, he said to Mariah, "Do you not think that Miss Tyler bears her burden well?"

Mariah smiled sweetly as she rose. "She is a saint, indeed."

Anne, feeling distinctly uncomfortable, said, "Thank you, but I bear it neither poorly nor well. It is simply there to be dealt with."

Troy patted her hand. "Nobly spoken."

"Anne is always well-spoken," said Mariah, again with a smile.

"Thank you, Mariah."

Anne could not decipher the strained expression on Mariah's face. However, she was beginning to regret bringing Troy along. His intrusion seemed to have cast a pall upon the latter part of the conversation. Perhaps, Mariah would be more herself the next time they spoke.

They bid her good-day and mounted the carriage.

Troy sat opposite her and watched her so intently that she began to feel discomfited.

"Mr. Fletcher, are you aware that you have been staring at me ever since we sat down?"

"Have I? Is it any wonder, when your beauty is enough to capture any man's heart and gaze?"

She blushed furiously. "That is kind, but hardly the case. And I find such close observation quite unnerving."

"My apologies. It is just that I admire you so intently. And I want to help you. I do not believe that you should have to carry such heavy burdens alone."

"I am not alone. Jeremy is a great comfort to me."

"Jeremy is a child, a responsibility for you. You need someone who can ease your burdens, someone who can give you a home and security. With that, you need not worry about what Mr. Tyler might do when he arrives."

"I would never marry simply to escape my fears, Mr. Fletcher."

"Of course not.

"Yet, surely it cannot have escaped your attention how madly I adore you. I have made no effort to hide it."

An image of Lord Westerfield flashed into her mind. She remembered how she had felt when they stood together gazing into each other's eyes. Perhaps there would never be any more than those brief moments together. Yet she knew she could live more happily on a lifetime of that memory than a lifetime with a man who did not stir her senses.

She took a deep breath. "I am flattered, truly I am..."

At her hesitation, he hastened to say, "Please do not delay your decision any longer. Please put me out of my misery by agreeing at once to become my wife."

He took her hands and gazed so intently at her that she could no longer think. Instinct took over and she blurted, "I cannot, sir. I do not wish to offend you in any way but I cannot marry you. I have tried to summon the feelings I require for marriage, but I cannot. And while I like you very well as a friend, I do not believe we are destined to marry."

He gripped her hands so tightly that her fingers ached. "What feelings must you summon? Surely there could be no better feeling than to own the heart of a man who has pledged to care for you and see to your comfort."

Anne tugged at her hands, yet failed to extract them.

"I am not insensitive to the value of your offer, Mr. Fletcher. But please trust me when I say that I cannot marry you. Now, as you are hurting my hands, would you please release me?"

For a moment, he stared at her while continuing to grip her fingers. It seemed to Anne as if he was deliberately extending her pain. And then, he released her, saying, "You are toying with me. You take pleasure in forcing me to declare my feelings for you while you deny me. I warn you that I will not be patient any longer. If you refuse me today, I will not come again to throw myself at your feet."

Anne stared at him, shocked by his accusation. "I assure you, Mr. Fletcher, that I have never toyed with you. In the past, I was not sure of my feelings, but now that I am sure, I am being completely honest."

As they pulled into Anne's drive, he fixed her with a cold stare. "Since you spurn me, I shall find someone more inclined toward my offer."

His words piqued her curiosity into wondering if he had someone in mind. Yet, she dared not ask. The cold fury in his green eyes reminded her of a caged panther she had seen once in India. He had paced the cage, growling and striking at anyone who came near as he watched with eyes that were steely and held no mercy, a predator.

The new driver helped Anne from her seat and waited politely for Troy to alight. Then he closed the door and trod slowly back to climb aboard and take the carriage and horses round to the stable.

Troy gave Anne a fleeting look of dismissal. "I suppose this is good-day, Miss Tyler, and good-bye. I shall not call again.'

"Good-bye, Mr. Fletcher."

Anne watched Troy stamp to the hired carriage. He spoke sharply to the driver and then settled himself inside. As they drove away, Anne found herself wondering if she had done the right thing. She knew she had thought with her heart and not her mind. Yet, what was she to do when her mind told her one thing and her heart another? To deny her heart would have felt too wrong. And yet, if Grandfather's nephew insisted she depart, would she regret her decision?

She felt exhausted as she entered the house. The entire morning had been confusing and draining. Mariah had behaved oddly and Troy had broken off their association. She regretted his disappointment on her behalf. Until his disturbing behavior in the carriage, he had been an engaging companion. She would miss his company.

She hung her bonnet on the rack inside the door and began to climb the stairs, thinking that perhaps a nap before lunch would ease the throbbing that had begun in her temples. She had just reached the top of the stairs when she heard Jeremy screaming as though he were being murdered.

She followed the commotion to find him engaged in a tug of war with his tutor. Jeremy bore a crimson mark where the man had struck him on the cheek. Between them, they held his treasured atlas.

Anne stepped between them, took hold of the book, and ordered them to let go. Jeremy stopped screaming and stared at her with wide eyes. The tutor, a tall wiry man brought his hands stiffly to his sides as though a skirmish with a nine-year-old was beneath him.

Anne looked from one to the other and said, "What is the meaning of this?"

"He tried to take away my book," Jeremy said as tears ebbed into his blue eyes.

"I caught this young man pouring through this worthless atlas when I had assigned him a whole morning's worth of mathematics to do. I thought a few weeks without it would teach him a lesson. When I demanded the book, he refused."

Jeremy caught at her hand. "Please, Anne, do not let him take it. It is Grandfather's book. Please say that he cannot have it."

Anne fixed Jeremy with a stern look. "Is it true that you have neglected your studies?"

Jeremy shook his head vigorously. "I finished my assignment. The papers are on the schoolroom desk. He told me to go and read while he corrected them."

"What do you have to say, sir? It seems he has finished his work." Anne demanded of the tutor.

"He did not want to come away from the atlas when I called him to correct his papers."

Jeremy shook his head. "It is not true. He did not call me."

The man stared coldly at the child. "You should not allow him to contradict his elders. It is a very bad habit in a child."

Anne spoke with rigid control. "But you have already contradicted yourself."

She glanced at the beautiful gold embossed illustrations on the cover of the atlas. Truly it was a remarkable book. Without a doubt, she knew who was telling the truth. She wondered if the tutor had intended to ever return the book.

She handed it to Jeremy. "Go into your room and read. I wish to speak with Mr. Ames."

"Thank you, Anne."

Jeremy took the book and fairly flew to his room.

Anne turned on the tutor. "You are perhaps the most unfeeling man I have ever known. This is Jeremy's most treasured possession, a gift from his grandfather and a memory of the man he loved. Yet you would take it from him on a whim. Pack your bags and be off immediately. We are no longer in need of your services."

"You have quite mistaken the situation. And you will ruin the boy by indulging his defiance."

"It is you who are mistaken. Jeremy is not and has never been a defiant child. He is obedient when the request is reasonable."

The man glowered. "Have it your way then. May it be on your conscience when he grows up wild and undisciplined."

He turned and strode briskly toward his room at the far end of the hallway.

Anne turned for her room, suddenly feeling shaken by the confrontation. Her knees felt as wobbly as a new colt as she pushed open her door. Tears burned behind her lids. At times like this, she hated the responsibility of being both mother and father to Jeremy. She worried constantly about making mistakes in his upbringing, mistakes that might ruin him forever. It did not help to be accused of just such negligence. And yet, it was obvious that Mr. Ames had coveted the book.

She fell across her bed and closed her eyes. She would not think about it anymore just now. She needed a rest badly. Perhaps everything would look better when she awoke.

Anne felt a light tapping on her arm. She groaned and shut her eyes tighter. Perhaps whoever was there would leave. She heard Jeremy say, "Anne, wake up. Mr. Ames has gone away."

She opened her eyes. "That is as it should be. I told him to do so."

"I am glad he is gone. He was a very nasty man."

Anne sat up. "You must not give your opinion unless it is asked for."

"But he was wicked. He always slapped me when I made mistakes in recitation."

Anne sighed. She could see that Jeremy was going to take a great deal of attention now that he had no one else to occupy his time. Perhaps she should look for another tutor. Yet, she had neither the time nor energy at present. She would wait until their future was settled and then see to a proper upbringing for her brother.

She glanced groggily at the mantel clock. It was nearly six-thirty, much later than she had realized. She must have slept for hours.

She gave Jeremy a gentle shove. "Go and dress for supper and you may eat with me tonight."

"All right."

Jeremy jumped off the bed and sprang for the door. "May I stay up late since I have no lessons tomorrow?"

"Perhaps a little late if you behave yourself very nicely."

"I shall."

He scurried off and Anne rang for Polly to assist her in her preparations.

Betsy came instead. She was wiping her eyes. "I hope you do not mind my coming, miss, but that no account little Polly took off with Mr. Ames. I thought they might have been carrying on with each other, but I hated to say anything until I was sure. And now it is too late and they have gone away."

Anne felt a moment of shock. "Polly? She has been with me for over two years. How could she do such a thing?"

"I do not know, miss."

A sinking feeling settled in Anne's stomach. Things were going all wrong since Grandfather had died. If only he were still here, he would have known how to best deal with Mr. Ames.

"I do not want to worry you, miss, but I caught Mr. Ames coming out of your grandfather's room. When I asked him what he was doing he told me it was none of my business."

She picked up a brush to brush out Anne's hair.

"He was in Grandfather's room?"

Betsy nodded. "Just before he left. I thought he might be getting something for the young master."

"That is not likely."

Anne leaped to her feet and scurried down the hall. She had not been inside Grandfather's room since he died. The memories were too painful. Yet she knew where he had kept everything of value. She checked the wardrobe, where nothing seemed to be amiss. Then she opened the drawers of the tall bureau that stood between the windows. The folded cravats were lying neatly inside the top drawer. She felt for the small velvet-lined box that held the diamond wedding ring that had been worn by her grandmother and then her mother.

She sighed with relief as she found the box. She drew it out and lifted the cover. The box was empty. She felt the blood drain from her face at the painful discovery. The ring that Jeremy was to have given to his future bride was gone.

She sank onto Grandfather's bed and burst into tears. Betsy caught up with her and stood miserably wringing her hands. "What is it, miss? What has happened?"

When Anne could choke out an answer, she showed Betsy the empty box. "I should have shown the wretched man out myself. This ring has been in our family for generations. And now it is gone."

Betsy began to sob, too. "I am glad your Grandfather is not alive to see this day. Oh, miss, what will you do?"

"What can I do? I do not know where he has taken it."

They sat thusly until Jeremy appeared, dressed for dinner. "Why Anne, you are not ready," he reproved.

She wiped her eyes and said, "Did Mr. Ames ever ask you to show him around this room?"

"Yes. Once he followed me when I came to get a book. He was very nice to me and asked to see the special things."

"What did you show him?"

"I showed him Grandfather's books and pipes and cans of tobacco. Sometimes I come in here to smell them. They remind me of Grandfather."

"Did you show him anything else?"

"I showed him mother's ring and the tiny white elephant Father sent Grandfather from India."

Anne frowned at Jeremy. She felt like shaking him. "You should never show someone's possessions to another person without permission."

Jeremy stared at her, his face confused. "But Grandfather is gone, Anne. How could I get his permission?"

Anne sighed in defeat. "I wish you had asked me. But it is too late now. You go down to supper and I will join you in a few moments."

Betsy helped her dress and quickly arranged her hair.

Jeremy was waiting at the table when she arrived. He arose like a proper young gentleman and her heart went out to her young brother who had not meant to do wrong.

"Why were you crying, Anne?"

She smiled sadly. "It seems you were right. Mr. Ames was a very bad man. He took Mother's ring today before he left."

Jeremy jumped to his feet and clenched his small hands. "I told you he was bad. I will ask the 'ostler to saddle my pony and go after him. I will make him give it back."

Anne's blue eyes shot him a warning. "You will do no such thing, Jeremy Tyler. Do you think getting yourself killed will bring me any comfort? You sit down right this minute and promise me that you will not do anything so foolish."

Jeremy stood stubbornly, wavering against making any such promise. Finally, his respect for his sister overpowered his desire for justice. "I promise I will not go right now. But sometime, when I am grown, I will find Mr. Ames and make him give back the ring."

"When you are grown, you may do as you please. But for now, you must do as I tell you."

Jeremy sat back down to supper. Yet neither of them had much appetite. They gave up and Anne took Jeremy into the parlor to read while she played on the pianoforte.

They had just seated themselves when a commotion arose from the kitchen and drifted toward the parlor. Someone was sobbing so dreadfully that Anne went to investigate.

She found Betsy supporting Polly. The girl was sobbing so uncontrollably that Anne ordered the butler to fetch her a brandy.

"What has happened, Polly? Why are you back?"

"I told her she had the nerve," said Betsy. "But all she does is cry."

Polly took the brandy and gratefully took a sip. When she had quieted a little, she fixed a watery gaze on Anne and began to explain.

CHAPTER FIVE

"PLEASE, MISS, YOU HAVE to believe that I did not know. If'n I had, I never would have had any part in it."

Anne frowned. "You are getting ahead of yourself. Start at the beginning and tell me what happened."

"It was Mr. Ames."

Tears rolled down her round cheeks and she took another sip of brandy.

"We borrowed a horse to ride to the village. We were to take a coach tomorrow to go to London to be married. When he showed me the ring, I thought it was for me. I asked how he could afford it."

She sniffed and continued. "He told me not to be so silly as to think it was for me. He had taken it from your Grandfather and decided he had best give it to a gentleman in exchange for payment for a job he did not get to finish, seeing as he was fired. He had arranged to meet the man along the dark bend in the road."

"What kind of job?"

"I think it had to do with the young master. Mr. Ames told the man he was sorry he did not get to take care of getting rid of him. He said he would have enjoyed it. It all sounded awful."

She took the rest of the brandy in a single gulp.

Anne took the girl by the shoulders. "Who was this man?"

Polly looked at her dully. "I could not see. He wore a scarf and it was dark."

"Where is Mr. Ames?"

Polly began to cry softly. "He is shot. The man shot him after he got off the horse. He might have shot me, too, except that I turned the horse and raced back here as fast as I could. Please say that you will not turn me out, Miss Tyler. I truly loved Mr. Ames and I thought he loved me."

Anne studied the girl and tried to make sense of what she had said. What worried her the most was, who would want to hurt Jeremy and why?

After a few moments, Polly said, "I nearly forgot. Mr. Ames let me wear the ring on the way to meet the man. I still had it on my finger when he was shot."

She pulled off the precious diamond and handed it to Anne.

Then she slumped in the chair and mumbled, "I told him it was wrong. Truly I did."

"Take her to bed, Betsy. She made a poor choice, but I do not believe she intended to do evil. Perhaps we can get more out of her in the morning."

She turned to Arthur. "Go and summon the 'ostler to get a party of men and ride out to where Mr. Ames was shot. If he is still alive, perhaps he can tell us what this is about."

Anne sent Jeremy to bed and then took the ring to her room for safekeeping. Then she went downstairs to await the return of the riders. It was nearly midnight when the men returned with word that there was no sign of Mr. Ames. Whoever had shot him must have buried the body in the woods.

Anne was left with no choice except to go to bed. Her heart was filled with anxiety for Jeremy. Someone had hired his tutor to harm him. And she had not the faintest idea of why.

She slept fitfully, worried that Mr. Ames might not be the only one hired to harm her brother. When she awoke, she went immediately to Jeremy's chamber to find him in peaceful slumber. His cheeks were rosy from the warmth of his bed. His black eyelashes curled on his cheeks. He looked so blissfully unaware of the danger that her heart ached to protect him. Yet, who could she trust?

Lord Westerfield leapt immediately to mind. He had no reason to wish either of them harm. Perhaps he might be able to tell her what she might do to protect her brother. She would send a note immediately asking him to come.

She hurried to her room to compose the missive.

Then, she rang for Betsy. "Tell Arthur to send a man immediately to Lord Westerfield. Give him this note and tell him it is an urgent matter."

"Yes, miss."

Anne picked at her breakfast while she waited impatiently for Lord Westerfield to arrive. At last, when it was nearly noon, she heard his voice in the entryway. She scurried to meet him.

His smile of greeting faded at the serious expression on her lovely face. She took his hands and drew him into the parlor.

"Thank goodness you got my note."

He drew his brows in puzzlement. "What note?"

"The one I sent this morning."

"Ah, I have been out visiting my tenants. I decided to drop by and see if you and Jeremy would like to come again to see the puppies. But I see that you must have a matter of a serious nature."

"I do indeed and I am most seriously in need of advice."

Lord Westerfield leaned forward, giving her his full attention. "Then I shall do my best to advise you."

When Anne had relayed everything she knew, he suggested they summon Polly to see what else might be learned. The girl was brought to stand before them. She spoke softly, nervously wringing her hands and repeating only what she had said the night before. And though Lord Westerfield gave her a thorough cross-examination, they were unable to learn anything more.

At last, Anne dismissed her to get back to her duties. She turned to Lord Westerfield. "What shall I do?"

He rubbed a hand across his chin. "We must find out what is behind the betrayal by Mr. Ames, though I must confess that I am at a loss as to how to begin. Perhaps I could start in the village and ask some questions to see if anyone else was approached to harm the boy."

"Would you? That would be a place to begin."

"In the meantime, do not let anyone new join your staff. And I would keep a good eye on Polly, even though she seems innocent enough of the worst of the affair."

"I shall ask Betsy to keep an eye on her, too."

They spoke a while longer over tea while Lord Westerfield laid out his strategy of who he might approach. Then with a promise to get back with her as soon as he had news, he made ready to depart. He took her hands in his and looked down into her eyes.

"If there is any way to get to the bottom of this, I will not stop trying until I do so."

She smiled at him. "You are kind, indeed."

He raised her hand and kissed it. "You have stolen my heart, Miss Tyler. There is very little I would not do for you."

He turned and strode away, shoulders broad and square. Anne watched him. And despite her worry, her heart felt as warm as her fingers from the memory of his kiss.

In the afternoon, she was summoned from the drawing-room where she was playing a game with Jeremy. She found Mariah awaiting her in the parlor. She took Mariah's hands and confessed, "I am so glad you are here. I have so much to tell you."

"I have something to tell you, too. Yet, I think it can wait as your news sounds most urgent."

"Indeed it is."

Anne rang for tea and then settled upon the settee with Mariah. Mariah listened in anticipation as Anne gave the unflattering account of Polly and Mr. Ames and of her fear that Jeremy was in danger.

Polly's blue eyes widened. "What a dreadful man. And you have no idea who hired him?"

"No idea at all. I sent men in search of him last night, but he had disappeared."

"This is shocking. What is to be done? Surely something must be done."

"Lord Westerfield has promised to ask in town if anyone was approached to do us evil."

"I hope he has success. Perhaps I could persuade Mr. Fletcher to do a similar service."

Anne shook her head. "I fear Mr. Fletcher will not want to do me any favors at the moment."

"Perhaps if I ask him, he will do it for me."

Mariah's pale cheeks flushed the becoming pink of a rose in bloom. "Why is that?"

The tea arrived and Mariah accepted a cup. Her blue eyes shone as she said, "Because he came yesterday and asked me to marry him."

She watched Anne closely as she rushed on to say, "I hope you are not hurt. I know we both thought that it was you that he loved. But then he came and told me that he has been enamored with me ever since the evening of the assembly. Oh, Anne, I have been in agony feeling such fondness for him and thinking that he would ask you. If only you knew how jealous I have been."

Now that she thought back, Anne recognized there had been a partiality on Mariah's part. Yet she did not believe it was returned by Mr. Fletcher. How could it be when he had declared his earnest love for Anne on the very same day?

Anne took a sip of tea and then asked, "Have you accepted?"

"Indeed. Mr. Fletcher insists that we be married before the next two weeks. He vows that he can wait no longer for me to become his wife. I have never been so happy. Mama and Papa are unsure, but they will soon consent."

Anne cast about for a gentle way to warn her friend, finally saying, "Perhaps you should find out more about him before you are wed."

Mariah scowled. "Why should I do that?"

"I can hardly put my finger on it," Anne admitted. "And yet, the stories of his past are sometimes flawed and inconsistent. And there is, on occasion, a bitterness about him, as though he carries the ghost of previous misfortune."

Mariah stared at her. "So you would counsel me not to marry him?"

Tears welled in her friend's eyes. Anne wished that she could push aside her suspicions and even the small twinge of jealousy at learning that Mr. Fletcher had replaced her so quickly in his affections.

"I would not counsel you to reject him but only to learn more about his past."

"But he has told me everything. He is the son of a wealthy London merchant. He had the finest of educations and has been to the continent on tour. He has a house in London and wishes to purchase another in the country. What more need I know?"

Anne uttered an incredulous laugh. "A great deal more, dear. Who is his father and what is his business? What has Mr. Fletcher done with himself since he came back from tour?"

Mariah's bosom heaved with indignation. "Why, he has helped his father, of course."

She waved a dismissing hand. "It is all I need to know. La, Anne, I thought you would be pleased that I was so happy. Instead, you have dampened my spirits with all of your doubts. Might it be that you are jealous? Perhaps you, too, expected Mr. Fletcher to ask for your hand."

Anne sighed, debating upon whether to tell her friend the truth. She decided that, if there was a true friendship between them, it must be based upon complete candor.

"He did ask me," she said softly. "He asked me yesterday on the way back from seeing you."

Mariah's small plump hand shook as she set down her teacup. "What a vengeful thing to say. You are doing all that you can to make him look bad. And now, you have cut me to the heart by telling me I was your second choice. Well, I do not care if I am the tenth choice. I shall marry my Mr. Fletcher and you will not ruin my excitement. I was going to ask you to stand up with me. Now, you shall be lucky to be invited to the wedding."

Anne leaned toward Mariah. "I did not mean to upset you. I simply thought that you should know."

"Why should I know? Just to satisfy your pride?"

Anne opened her mouth to protest. Before she could do so, Mariah rose and said, "I shall be going now. And I shall not call again. I suggest you save yourself the trouble of calling upon me. I shall be very busy planning my wedding."

She turned a deaf ear to Anne's apologies as she swept out of the room. Anne was left alone to wonder at the circumstances that had caused her to lose her friend. Perhaps she should not have been so forthright. After all, the way things had gone lately, she had few friends to spare. Yet, she knew she would do no differently if she had it to do again. If she had failed to express her doubts to Mariah, she would have been less than a friend.

Mr. Westerfield appeared later in the afternoon. She met with him in the drawing-room, eager to discover what he had learned. He sat very close to her and took her hand. He shook his head as he said, "I have asked all around. No one admits to being propositioned to harm the boy. Perhaps Polly misunderstood the conversation."

Anne frowned, looking doubtful. "I suppose it is possible. But why was Mr. Ames bringing the man the ring?"

"Mayhaps they were to sell it and split the money. The murderer may have found that Mr. Ames was making away with it alone."

"I suppose that could be true."

He saw her uncertainty and wanted to ease her mind. "It must be true. What possible reason could anyone have for harming Jeremy?"

"I admit that I cannot think of any."

"Then we must assume that the murder was a matter between two thieves. Your brother is safe and all will be well. But if it will make you feel better, I shall keep a close eye on him when we go to see the puppies. It will do you good to get out after such a shock to your nerves."

"Will it now?" She smiled at him impishly, feeling comforted by his reassurances.

"Yes. It is just what is required. I have already sent word to Jeremy, so he will be most disappointed if you refuse."

He ran a finger down the line of her chin and she knew that she would be disappointed as well.

"I shall not refuse," she said, softly.

He gazed deeply into her eyes. She sat mesmerized, drowning in the inky depths of his scandalously dark eyes. She caught her lip in her teeth as she felt her heart hammering against her ribs and knew that she was helpless against the effect he had upon her.

Suddenly Jeremy bounded into the room. "Are you ready, Anne?" Lord Westerfield says I might go and see my puppy."

Anne thought about correcting him in the assumption that he would surely get the pup. She decided just as quickly against it. Let him enjoy his dream and if it must be postponed, she would deal with it then.

"I need only get my bonnet," she assured her impatient young brother.

When she had secured her ribands, Lord Westerfield escorted them to his carriage. "You know, of course, that my father is anticipating your company at tea. He talked of it for hours the last time you came."

Anne smiled. "He is a delightful man and I should be most happy to join him."

"He will be pleased, also. He likes you very well, indeed."

Lord Westerfield rested a gaze upon her that conveyed his approval. Anne flushed and wondered that he continued to seek her company. She considered herself a serious sort, unlike the flirtatious girls who usually obtained men's attention. And though she had never felt the slightest desire to perfect the art of flattery or coquettishness, she had considered herself at a disadvantage with the girls who did. And yet here was a plainspoken young lord who did not seem to find it a fault. And this intrigued her all the more.

They arrived at the stable where Jeremy rushed ahead to see the puppies.

"He will be surprised how much they have grown in the last few days," said Lord Westerfield.

"I suppose puppies and boys both grow quickly. I shall have to have new trousers made for Jeremy in the fall."

"You do a wonderful job looking after him."

Lord Westerfield gave her a warm smile that put a glow in his dark eyes.

"I do my best. Yet, I know that I do not always make the best decisions."

His smile lingered. "From what I know of you, your best will be quite sufficient."

They joined Jeremy to watch the puppies tumble and play.

"Look, mine is the biggest of all. He'll be a fine strong dog, will he not, Lord Westerfield?" Jeremy asked.

The puppies' mother came over for attention and Lord Westerfield scratched her behind the ear. "He will be the best of all."

"When may we train him to hunt?'

Lord Westerfield laughed. "It will be a few weeks still."

"I shall teach him to be the best hunting dog ever."

"I am sure you shall."

They let Jeremy tumble with the puppies for a while. Then Lord Westerfield told Anne, "I think you would feel better if Jeremy came inside to take his tea in the kitchen, would you not?"

"Yes. I cannot think of leaving him alone in the stable. I am afraid it will take me a few days to recover from my fear on his behalf."

"Then he shall come in with us."

Jeremy balked when Anne told him that he must leave the puppies. Yet at her insistence, he bid his favorite pup good-bye and drew some comfort from the cakes that were promised to go with his tea.

While Jeremy skipped ahead, Anne and Lord Westerfield walked together to the house. On the way, Anne stopped to admire the lilacs that grew along the path. Their fragrance gave off a heavenly scent that reminded her of the cologne her mother had worn. She was gripped by a nostalgia that brought tears to her eyes. She blinked quickly and saw him watching her.

"Silly is it not, how a certain fragrance can bring back memories. These flowers remind me of my mother."

He nodded sympathetically and said, "It is not at all silly. I do not remember much about my mother. I do recall that she wore rose-scented cologne. And I can vaguely remember the sound of her laughter and that her hand was soft when she touched my cheek."

Anne nodded. "And yet it does no good to look back. Perhaps it is best not to think of it."

She wiped her eyes and straightened her shoulders. The strain of the last two days had taken a toll. She looked up at Lord Westerfield and said, "Please forgive me. I am not usually given to moods of nostalgia.

"There is nothing to forgive. You do not always have to be strong. At least not with me."

To her surprise, he wrapped her gently in his arms and hugged her to his chest. Anne knew she should pull away and yet she felt so comforted by his solid body and strong arms that she could not will herself to move. His embrace felt like a fortress of protection, a hide-away from all that troubled her. And right now, she desperately craved a refuge from her storms.

Jeremy called back to them from around the hedge. "Are you coming?"

Lord Westerfield released her and Anne straightened her bonnet, squared her shoulders and prepared to resume her responsibilities. He watched her, admiring the resiliency housed in her small form. Most women he knew would have taken to their chambers for weeks after so many mishaps. Overtaken by the vapors, they would have languished dramatically and soaked in the sympathy of friends. It seemed that Anne had never had, nor desired such attention. Instead, she focused her attention and protection upon those she loved. What an honor it would be to be counted among those few. And to return her affection would take no effort at all. Admiring her as he did, he felt a fierce burning to lavish his attention and protection upon her.

He let his imagination drift as they walked along the path. It would be lovely to have a wife such as Anne in his house, someone he could talk to and respect her opinions. Already, he loved spending time with her. Yet her reserve made it difficult to tell how she felt about him. Still, he took encouragement in the fact that she had not pulled away when he held her.

They walked companionably to the house. After directing Jeremy to the kitchens, Anne and Lord Westerfield joined the elder lord in the parlor where he awaited them, sitting in a straight chair at the tea table, a red wool blanket resting across his lap. He beamed broadly at the sight of Anne. "My dear you are like a rare flower. Is it not nice to have a woman in the house?" he asked his son.

"It is nice to have Miss Tyler."

"Yes, of course. Miss Tyler is special. She is not giddy, but a sensible young woman. I most enjoy your company, my dear."

Anne smiled. "I thank you for the compliment. However, I am afraid I must admit to occasions of behaving in as silly a manner as the next girl."

The young lord drew out her chair and seated her at the table. As he bent down, he whispered in her ear. "I should pay dearly for the opportunity to see you giddy."

She flushed slightly and turned her attention to the elder lord. "Have you been well, sir?"

"As well as these old bones allow. I am always better as the day wears on. Of course, having you for company takes my mind off my aches."

She smiled. "I am glad of that."

When the tea arrived, Anne offered to pour it. When she handed the elder lord his cup, she watched his gnarled fingers struggle to grip it. It was no wonder he complained of aches. Judging from the swollen joints of his hands, she was not surprised that daily tasks caused him such misery.

But, seeming not to want to dwell upon his health, he was eager to talk about how Anne was getting on. She told about the letter from her uncle and about the strange goings-on of Mr. Ames."

He frowned and clucked his tongue. Then banging his cup onto his saucer, he said, "If there are thieves in town, we must get to the bottom of this."

He turned to his son. "You must ride in and make inquiries, or next thing we know, this outlaw will be bribing servants all over Sussex to steal from their employers."

"I did that already. No one in town could tell me anything about the man who hired Ames."

"Well, I do not like it. I certainly do not like it," declared the elder lord, his dark eyes flashing. "Something must be done.

"I shall keep an eye out, Father. The man who started this is probably long away by now. But I have asked that if anyone sees or hears anything suspicious, they would let me know."

"I hope he is caught, and when he is..." he stopped, suddenly remembering Anne was with them.

"I hope he is properly punished," he said. "At least the girl had the ring and was able to return it."

"I am grateful for that," Anne said.

Young Lord Westerfield drew the discussion onto more pleasant topics. They discussed the weather and the gardens and the new vicar who had recently arrived in town.

"That reminds me. I have just had word that Miss Sawyer is to marry Mr. Fletcher," Anne said. "I must confess that I was surprised by the speed of the match."

Lord Westerfield nodded. "He was the man who accompanied you to the assembly. I remember him well. I was jealous that he was your escort and I was not."

"You need not have been jealous. I never felt any special attachment to Mr. Fletcher, especially since he so readily transfers his affection. I am simply surprised that Miss Sawyer accepted."

"Perhaps she favored him for some time, but did not tell you due to being your friend."

"I suppose that must be the truth. I can think of no other reason for her to accept him so quickly."

The young lord, seeming pleased that Mr. Fletcher was out of her life, said, "I wish them both happiness."

"As do I," replied Anne, truly hoping she was wrong in her intuition regarding Mr. Fletcher.

They finished their tea and took leave from the elder Lord Westerfield after extracting a promise from Anne to return soon. They found Jeremy happily licking pudding from a bowl in the kitchen.

"May I see the puppy once again before we leave? Please, Anne."

She frowned. "We have taken enough of Lord Westerfield's time already. I am sure he has business that demands his attention."

Lord Westerfield ruffled Jeremy's hair. "I do have business in town this afternoon. However, a quick stop to bid the puppy good-bye will not unduly delay me."

They stopped at the stables where Jeremy hugged the wriggling pup. Anne insisted that he did not tarry long and soon they were clattering away toward home with Lord Westerfield. Before they arrived, Anne said, "I have come to tea twice now. I will feel most inhospitable if you do not accept an invitation to a picnic in our park."

"I should be delighted to accept, only tell me when to come."

"Would you be available at one-o'clock next Friday? "

"I am available and shall be pleased to accept your hospitality."

"Then I am very glad indeed."

Anne's smile faded as they rounded the curve of trees and saw a couch pulling away from the front of the house.

"Look, Anne, someone has just arrived," Jeremy said.

"It must be Grandfather's nephew," she replied.

CHAPTER SIX

.. ⚬ܓ ..

IN THE ENJOYMENT SHE had taken in visiting the Westerfield estate, she had nearly forgotten about Mr. Tyler's planned arrival. As the reality of his coming registered in her mind, she felt a nervous flutter in her stomach. She clutched Lord Westerfield's arm. His stalwart strength comforted her now that a man she had never met was the guardian of Grandfather's estate, a man who had the power to eject her or allow her to stay.

She turned to Lord Westerfield and asked. "Will you not go in with me?"

His heart lurched to see her pale face and trembling lips. Yet determination to meet whatever lay ahead shone in her clear blue eyes.

"I should be glad to do so if it would help," he replied.

He assisted her from the carriage and accompanied her as she walked, head held high, to the door. Arthur admitted them and announced the arrival of the new master. "He is in the parlor, miss, and has requested to see you upon your return."

Anne brushed Jeremy's hair off his forehead, straightened his shirt and smoothed her skirts. Then, with a deep breath, she plunged them all into the parlor. The new Mr. Tyler was just taking tea. He rose when he saw them and Anne noticed that he was a thin man, tall and rather shabbily dressed in a gray waistcoat that was faded from wear and trousers that were frayed at the cuffs. His hair was gray and quite sparse. His lips were thin in his narrow face and he had the dark blue eyes characteristic of the Tyler family.

Anne curtsied and then gave him a tentative smile. "You must be Grandfather's nephew. I am Anne Tyler, his granddaughter and this is my brother, Jeremy."

She glanced up at her companion. "This is our friend and neighbor, Lord Westerfield."

Mr. Tyler bowed. "It is a pleasure to meet all of you. Please, will you not join me at tea? It has been a long trip and I have had little in the way of sustenance."

"We have had our tea, but perhaps we might visit while you have yours," Anne said.

Mr. Tyler nodded. "An excellent idea. Please sit down. I would like to get to know my relatives."

Jeremy joined Mr. Tyler on the settee while Anne and Lord Westerfield were seated in chairs opposite the settee. After a moment of silence, Anne said, "Have you not brought your family, Mr. Tyler?"

"I have no family. My wife is dead and I have no children. And while I was distressed to hear of your grandfather's death, I look forward to having a family again."

"You mean Anne does not have to leave?" Jeremy blurted.

Anne sent him a look of stern reprimand for speaking out.

Mr. Tyler stared at the child in puzzlement. "Why should she have to leave?"

Seeing Anne's disapproval, Jeremy turned his attention to Mr. Tyler, knowing it would be rude not to answer now. "She thought that you might not want her here and might send her away now that you are my guardian. But someday, the house will be mine and I could have her come back."

Anne felt as though she would die of embarrassment.

Yet, Mr. Tyler threw back his head and laughed. Then he said, "Why should she leave only to come back? Would you not like her to stay with you?"

"Oh, yes. Only Anne was worried you would not let her."

"I am not such an ogre as to throw my relatives from their home. Of course, Anne may stay."

Despite Jeremy's lack of manners, Anne breathed a sigh of relief. She would not have to use up her pension on a new place to live. Nonetheless, she made a mental note to speak to Jeremy about his boldness with his elders.

Mr. Tyler devoured a small tea cake and turned his attention to Westerfield. "And you, sir, are you not the son of the Viscount of Westerfield? I met him once many years ago."

"I am, sir. I have recently come from living with my uncle in London so that I might assist my father."

"And how is your father? Is he in health?"

"Not as he would like to be. He has pains in his arms and legs that make it difficult for him to get around as he was accustomed."

"That is too bad. He is a fine man. No doubt you take after him."

"Thank you, sir. I should be pleased if I do."

They sat a moment and then Westerfield asked, "And you, sir, what did you do in London?"

Mr. Tyler grimaced. "At one time, I owned a business selling coal and oil. I had a nice home and did well. And then, unfortunate circumstances came along and my business began to suffer. I was forced to sell it a few years ago and live on the profit ever since."

"I am sorry to hear it," Anne said. She wondered from the look of him if his profits had nearly given out. In that case, he needed a home as much as she and Jeremy. Her curiosity was piqued as to the source of his misfortune. Yet, whatever the reason, she hoped he would be happy here.

Changing the subject, Westerfield asked, "Are you much given to hunt?"

"I have had little opportunity of late. I used to enjoy it as a boy."

"Perhaps you would like to join me when you are rested and settled. I plan to shoot for pheasants in a day or so."

"I should be very pleased to shoot with you if you can overlook my lack of practice."

"I am sure it will come back to you."

Anne sent Jeremy a warning look as she saw him scoot to the edge of his seat, eager to tell about his puppy. Westerfield noted his excitement and said, "Young Jeremy has just picked out a fine pup to be trained for retrieving. Perhaps if Miss Tyler does not object, he might come along to see what his dog will learn."

"May I Anne? Oh, please," Jeremy begged.

Anne looked panicked. "I will have to think about it. After all, there will be shooting. I should not want you to get hurt."

"I promise to keep a keen eye on him. He will never be in any danger," Westerfield promised.

Anne locked her gaze upon him, her face pinched in worry. "Are you *sure* he would not be in danger?"

"I am completely sure."

"Very well."

She turned to Jeremy. "You must promise to listen to Lord Westerfield and obey him at all times."

"I promise."

Westerfield felt his heart warm at the trust she had shown in him by agreeing to let Jeremy go. He knew how much the boy meant to her and how worried she had been for his safety. He must be making inroads to her heart if she would allow him charge of her beloved brother.

Westerfield glanced at the mantel clock. "It has been a pleasure to meet you and now I must go. I have some business in the village."

"And a pleasure to meet you, also. I shall look forward to our hunt," replied Mr. Tyler.

"Please excuse me for a moment while I see Lord Westerfield out," said Anne.

When they reached the door, Westerfield knew by her furrowed brow that something had displeased her. Her blue eyes shot a warning as she said, "Lord Westerfield, in the future, I would appreciate it if you would ask me before you invite my brother on an outing. I hate having to disappoint him when he has set his hopes upon something, but I shall do as I think best. If anything should arouse my fears on his behalf, I shall rescind my permission."

Westerfield felt as though his patience was being stretched. "Nothing is going to happen to Jeremy and you are doing your brother a disservice by such protective behavior. He is a solid young chap, sturdy and forthright. Do you want to make him weak and fearful?"

"Of course not," she sputtered. "But he is my responsibility and not yours and I shall decide what he does and does not do. So I will repeat my request. In the future, will you speak to me before you invite him on outings?"

Westerfield felt sorely tested and thoroughly out of sorts by Anne's insistence upon having him humor her ridiculous fears. Nor was he used to having young women dictate his behavior. In doing so, she had insulted his judgment and hurt his pride.

He scowled down at her and said, "If you are going to be so peevish, perhaps I had best not invite the boy for anything at all. You can lock him in his chambers and serve his food through a slit and keep him there until he is an old man withered and pale from lack of sunlight."

Anne could not believe the unfairness of his ridiculous suggestion. She did not want to deprive Jeremy of opportunity nor did she want to lock him away from the world. She simply wanted to be sure there was no immediate threat. Was it not right to be cautious until she knew?

She met his angry gaze with an equally irate stare. "You have no idea what it is like to be responsible for someone else. Jeremy is all I have left in the world and if there is any possibility of danger, think what you will of me, I shall not risk him. And if you do not like it, you need not feel obliged to invite either of us to anything."

"Perhaps I shall not. I will leave you to hide in your house and jump at every shadow and hear danger in every footstep."

Anne raised her chin, though her heart was bruised and her throat was tight. "If that is how you feel, then I shall bid you a good day."

Her small face was so hard set that she might have been carved from stone. She pressed her lips into a tight line and straightened her body to her full petite height.

He bowed. "Good day, Miss Tyler. Pray, do not trouble yourself any further with me. I shall be off and let you get back to your vigil."

He strode from the house and swung into the carriage, which clattered away down the drive and was soon out of sight.

Anne swiped at angry tears and told herself that she did not care what he thought of her or whether he ever called again. She had managed to take care of herself and Jeremy thus far without the help of Lord Westerfield and she would continue to do so. After all, she had known him too short a time to make any firm attachment. And yet, her mind balked at this untruth and it took her a full five minutes to compose herself enough to return to the parlor.

When she entered the room, she found Mr. Tyler laughing heartily at a story Jeremy was telling him about the monkeys in India. Despite her battered spirits, she smiled as she remembered the funny imps that chattered from trees and occasionally scampered in through open windows.

Mr. Tyler wiped mirthful tears from his eyes and told Anne. "Your brother is an amusing young man. We have had a delightful chat and I cannot wait to hear more about India."

"Would you like to see a book that Grandfather gave me? It has ever so many wonderful drawings of tigers," Jeremy said.

Mr. Tyler smiled. "I should love to see it, perhaps tomorrow. Now, I am tired from my journey and I should like to go up and rest."

"We have had a room prepared for you. I hope that it will be adequate. Of course, it is your choice if you should like to move to another after you have had a look about the house," Anne said.

"I am sure you have chosen well for me and that I will be entirely comfortable."

Anne turned to Jeremy. "Go and tell Betsy that Mr. Tyler wishes to be escorted to his room."

Jeremy hopped off the settee and scurried off to find Betsy.

Anne smiled at Mr. Tyler. "It is very kind of you to allow me to remain in the house. We shall endeavor not to cause you any reason to change your mind."

Mr. Tyler rose and gave Anne a long look. Then he said, "I should not want either of you walking on tenterhooks, worried to make a sound or utter an opinion for fear of being thrown out. I want you to go about just as you are accustomed to. I assure you, I welcome both the company and the stimulation of having young people in the house."

"Thank you, sir. You are kind, indeed."

He bowed gallantly as Betsy appeared to escort him to his room.

Anne turned to Jeremy and said, "I am going to have a rest. I want you to remain inside the house until I arise. Then, perhaps, we shall have a walk about the garden."

"But I want to go out and look at the goldfish in the pond. I promised Grandfather I would check on them. And if I am lucky, I may catch a frog."

Anne shook her head. "We will do those things after a rest. For now, you may go to the kitchen and visit Cook or you may look at your books."

Jeremy plopped onto the settee in a pout. Yet, he did not argue. Anne's tone had already told him that there would be no use.

Anne plodded up the stairs, feeling nearly desperate to be alone. Her emotions were in a whirl and she wanted the comfort and safety of her room, with its rose print wallpaper and thick comforting rug.

She sank onto her bed and sighed. Things had begun so promisingly this morning. They had enjoyed a lovely time with Lord Westerfield and his father. And now, things had gone dreadfully wrong.

She wondered dismally if the quarrel would be the end of the friendship, a friendship that had come to mean a great deal to her.

She repeated the conversation in her mind and wondered what she could have done to prevent the disagreement. She wished she had not felt driven to speak her mind. Yet, when she could think of nothing she could have changed, she decided that she had been in the right in her demand and that Lord Westerfield had shown an unbecoming arrogance. Nonetheless, she felt hurt and angry that he so easily dismissed her concern.

She lay down and shut her eyes. No matter how she tried, it was some time before she could get the scowling image of Lord Westerfield, his dark eyes flashing, out of her mind. For even in his irritation, he presented a handsome figure of a man, a man striving for patience even when he was annoyed. Despite her grievance against him, she found much in him to respect.

She awoke late in the afternoon and rang for tea. When it arrived, she found that she had very little appetite. She nibbled at a sandwich and then sent the tray away. Feeling too restless to remain in her chamber, she decided a walk would do her good.

She donned her slippers and bonnet and set out the front door, walking toward the lane that led to town. She paused when she had walked a mile and decided she had no interest in going into the village. She started to turn for home and then changed her mind. She wondered if it would be possible to make amends with Mariah. She hated the damage done to their friendship when their last conversation had gone so very ill. Perhaps if she paid a visit, things could be restored.

She continued along to the lane that wound to Mariah's home. With each step, she breathed the delightfully sweet scent of honeysuckle in full bloom. Squirrels chattered as they scampered between the trees that lined the lane. Dogs barked in the distance and a lark sang his song from a stone fence. The azure sky supplied pasture to a fluffy cloud of white sheep.

Anne smiled and felt her spirits revive. It was a beautiful afternoon, the sort of afternoon where nothing could go wrong. She would talk things out with Mariah and all would be well.

She reached the austere, gray-bricked house and prepared to knock on the door. Her hand froze as she saw Mariah appear from the garden behind the house, holding a deep red rose. Anne flushed as red as the flower when she saw that Mariah was not alone. She was accompanied by Mr. Fletcher.

She desired to flee. When Mariah gave her an icy smile, she realized it was too late.

"Why, look, Mr. Fletcher, we have company."

"Indeed, I believe it is Miss Tyler come to call."

He bowed in front of Anne.

Mariah frowned and said, "I do wonder what she might want."

"Perhaps she will tell you. I shall leave you ladies to your visit. I have business inside which needs my attention."

With another bow, Mr. Fletcher walked past them and entered the house.

Mariah eyed Anne suspiciously. "What are you doing here?"

Anne swallowed, feeling unsettled by the awkwardness of the situation. Yet knowing she must explain, she said, "I felt distressed that you were upset. I hoped to make amends and restore our friendship."

Mariah gave her a haughty smile. "I doubt we have anything in common anymore. You are both untitled and unmarried while I, at least, am married."

Anne stared at her in disbelief. "How could this be?"

Mr. Fletcher and I stole away yesterday and were married. He said he could not bear to be apart from me any longer. Mama and Papa were not pleased, but they are accepting it. Perhaps we will have a larger ceremony later."

"And you are living here?"

"For the time being. Mr. Fletcher says it may take a little time to find the perfect house. He does not want to settle for a small estate."

Anne caught her lip. She would have thought in the time he had been here, Mr. Fletcher would know whether or not there was anything to his liking. Yet she dared not say this to Mariah. Instead, she said, "I hope you shall both be very happy. Perhaps you might like to come for tea in a few days."

Mariah gave a disdainful shake of her head. "Married women are very busy. I shall not be as you are, with time to fritter away."

The cutting remarks stung, leaving Anne feeling unworthy and dismissed. As she desired no further conversation with Mariah, she said, "I must go and leave you to your many tasks. You are welcome, should you ever have the time."

Mariah bestowed a stiff smile. "Thank you, but I fear that I shall not."

"Good-day, Mariah."

"Good-day."

Mariah might choose to cut her, but it did not change her opinion of Mr. Fletcher.

She turned and walked back down the lane. The day did not seem at all cheerful anymore. She did not notice the birds and squirrels, nor take the least comfort from the scent of honeysuckle. She wished only to get home and nurse her wound.

She followed the lane until the tall turrets of her home welcomed her like an old friend. She felt some of her tension melt away. At least one thing had gone well today. Mr. Tyler had spoken kindly to her about desiring their company in the house. And that was worth a great deal to Anne. And as long as she had this house, with its memories of Grandfather, she would always have a place to find comfort.

When she got inside, Arthur gave her the message that Mr. Tyler was too fatigued to come down and would be taking his supper in his room that evening. Anne nodded, realizing that she felt relieved.

While he was a pleasant man and she was grateful to him, she did not know him well enough yet to feel relaxed in his company. Now that she was free to plan the evening, she decided to invite Jeremy to supper in her room. They would eat and play some of his favorite games. That was sure to make him happy as well as cheer her from her melancholy mood; for Jeremy's lively enthusiasm always lifted her spirits when they were low.

She found Jeremy in the library pouring over a large dusty volume. He glanced up accusingly and said, "I have been waiting to go to the pond. You said we might when you awoke."

"I did promise and I am sorry to have taken so long."

She did not mention her walk to Mariah's house.

"We can go now. And would you like to have supper with me tonight? Just the two of us. We can play a few games before you go to bed."

Jeremy's eyes lit. "Yes. But what about Mr. Tyler?"

"He is taking supper in his room."

Jeremy grinned as he sprung to his feet. He grabbed Anne's hand and began to haul her towards the French doors that led to the garden. "Hurry. We do not want to waste any time."

Anne laughed and allowed him to tug her along until they were both flushed and out of breath. At the far end of the garden, Jeremy knelt along the rock wall of the small pond and peered into the water. A fat orange fish swam to the surface and Jeremy grinned.

"This is Willy. He is telling me hello."

Anne leaned to peer into the murky water. "Hello, Willy. Are you alone in there?"

"No. The last time I counted, we had eight more."

She dusted the rocks and sat on the ledge of the pond. "Grandfather would be proud of the way you care for the fish."

Jeremy sat beside her on the ledge. "They make me remember Grandfather and the way we came here together."

Anne looked across the pond to the grove of old oak trees that grew just past the clearing. "It is a lovely place to spend time."

"You can come out here any time you like."

She smiled at Jeremy. "Thank you. Perhaps I shall come again. But this will always be your special place and will always remind you of Grandfather."

They remained awhile longer while Jeremy fed the fish and grabbed at a fat frog that he was unable to catch. Finally, it was time to go in to supper.

"Bring your maps and we shall play a game," Anne reminded him.

They spent a pleasant evening eating a light supper of baked pheasant and boiled potatoes. They took turns quizzing each other with the maps and Jeremy won every turn.

"I must study before we play again," Anne said when it was time to send Jeremy to bed.

"Then I shall not be able to beat you."

Anne laughed. "Even if I study, you shall always be able to beat me."

Exhausted from the day, Anne prepared for bed. She wished only to seek respite in the blessedness of sleep. Yet for some time she tossed and turned, wishing she could talk to Lord Westerfield about what had happened with Mariah. She felt a deep loss, an ache in her heart, which made her realize just how much she had enjoyed his company. She wondered if he felt the same about her.

When she finally drifted to sleep, she was awakened in the morning by voices just outside her room. She recognized loud protests from Jeremy interspersed by murmured words from Mr. Tyler.

She threw a wrap around her and hurried to investigate, determined to discover what could have caused such a scene. She was unprepared for the sight that greeted her when she opened her door.

CHAPTER SEVEN

. . ∽⊷ . .

ANNE PAUSED TO SEE a younger thinner version of her grandfather standing in the hall. He was wearing Grandfather's morning coat and his soft gray trousers. And he carried the familiar cane and favorite bowler hat. He looked at Anne in some distress as Jeremy began to shout, "Tell him he cannot wear Grandfather's things. They do not belong to him. Tell him, Anne."

Anne came out of her shock and dashed to kneel beside Jeremy. "They may as well belong to him, dear. You must stop making such a fuss. Those clothes are no use to Grandfather now."

Jeremy stopped protesting and began to sniffle.

Anne glanced up at Mr. Tyler. "I am sorry. It must have been a shock to him to see you in Grandfather's things."

"I am the one who is sorry. I did not mean to upset the young man. If I could do so, I would leave them be and not cause such distress. But necessity does not allow me to do so. Perhaps if I explain, he will understand why I do not humor him. Will you both join me for breakfast and hear what I must say?"

"We should be happy to do so. I will dress immediately and come down."

Mr. Tyler nodded. With a regretful glance at Jeremy, who refused to meet his eyes, he trod down the stairs.

Anne turned to her brother. "You must promise that you will not make a fuss while I go and dress. You will sit quietly and wait for me. Do you understand?"

Jeremy nodded. He looked up at Anne and there were tears in his eyes. "Do you not care about Grandfather anymore?"

"Of course I care. But Grandfather would want Mr. Tyler to use his clothes. Do you think he would rather see them go to waste?"

Jeremy shook his head. He wore a look of defeat. "I suppose not."

Anne patted his shoulder. "Stay still and wait for me. I will only be a few moments."

Anne washed at the blue china washbowl and hurried to don a pale pink summer dress. The sleeves were puffed and adorned with pink satin bows. Betsy bustled in to button the tiny row of back buttons and to smooth her dark curls into submission. When she was finished, Anne asked, "How is Polly working out as downstairs maid?"

"Just lovely, miss. I think she still feels so bad about her mistake that she is meek as a mouse."

"I am glad to hear it. I kept her on because I did not believe she ever meant to do us any harm."

"I am sure she did not, miss."

"Nonetheless, keep an eye on her, Betsy. Let me know if she takes up with any new men."

"I will keep a close eye on her," Betsy promised.

"Thank you."

Anne found Jeremy sitting dispiritedly in the hall outside her door. She reached her hand to him. "Let us join Mr. Tyler for breakfast and hear what he would tell us."

Jeremy took her hand and walked beside her down the stairs. He sighed and said, "I like Lord Westerfield. When will he come again?"

Anne felt as though a knife had turned in her heart.

"I do not know when we will see Lord Westerfield."

She tried to keep her tone light. She did not want Jeremy to suspect that something was amiss as she was in no mood to answer his questions.

"He said I might go hunting with him. And I want to see my puppy."

"Lord Westerfield is a busy man. Yet, I am sure he has not forgotten his promise regarding the puppy."

Anne clenched her jaw until it ached.

Jeremy did not notice. "I am sure he has not forgotten. Still, I want to teach my puppy to hunt. So, I hope Lord Westerfield comes again soon. Do you not hope so, too?"

"Yes. That would be lovely. Now, put on your best manners and greet Mr. Tyler politely."

They entered the sunny room beside the back gardens where breakfast awaited them. The sideboard was stacked with sweetbreads, eggs, sausages, and fruit. Though the smell was delectable, Anne found that her appetite had deserted her, due in no small part to Jeremy's mention of Lord Westerfield.

"Good morning, Mr. Tyler." Jeremy's manner was polite if a bit formal.

Nonetheless, Anne was proud of him for making the effort.

After Anne and Mr. Tyler exchanged greetings, they all chose their breakfast and settled at the table. Mr. Tyler, having piled his plate, dug in with relish. Anne could not help but wonder what had kept him so thin if he was in the habit of eating so voraciously. But perhaps he was still recovering from the strain of the trip.

Between bites, he began to tell them his story. "You see, Jeremy, I would be happy not to touch your grandfather's clothes if I had fitting clothes of my own. I hate to upset you, for I am fond of you both, though I have known you for a very short time. Yet you must understand that a proper gentleman of an estate cannot be seen in the wardrobe I possess."

Jeremy eyed him suspiciously. "What is wrong with it?"

"My clothes are old. They are patched and faded. Life has not been kind to me, though much of it is my fault."

Anne saw Jeremy open his mouth to ask another question and she quickly cut him off. "You do not have to explain unless you wish. We have no right to question your past."

Mr. Tyler shook his head. "I think you deserve to know a bit about my background. You see, for a time, I was a very bitter man who squandered his money on drinking and gambling. I owned a prosperous business at one time, but my habits led me to lose it."

As tears pricked Ann's eyes, she whispered, "I am sorry."

"Do not pity me. It was my choice., though I took no blame at the time. I do not know if I would have come to my senses had I not met a minister who made me see the folly of my waste. He preached to me and I listened. I stopped destroying myself with too much liquor. It was too late to do anything about my financial losses. By then, I lived in a small drafty room and could barely afford to eat. Then, I got word that your Grandfather had died and I had been named guardian of the estate."

Anne and Jeremy stared at him, unable to think of anything to say.

He continued. "Though I am deeply sorry for the loss of your grandfather, I must say that it was my financial salvation. I could not have held out much longer."

"Had you no one to help you? No relatives or family in London?" Anne asked.

Mr. Tyler shook his head. A look of pain passed across his face. "That is another story. Perhaps I shall tell it to you one day. It is not a happy tale and certainly not for Jeremy's young ears. Still, I did want him to understand that it was my need and not greed that drove me to procure your grandfather's clothes. Do you understand, Jeremy?"

"Yes. You needed them because you were poor."

"That is right. Will it upset you if I wear them?"

Jeremy shook his head. "Anne is right. It will not help our grandfather to save them. I suppose he would want you to have them."

Mr. Tyler smiled. "Thank you, Jeremy. I shall feel much better about using them now."

Anne felt her admiration grow for Mr. Tyler. He had owed neither of them an explanation. Yet, he had taken pains to win Jeremy's approval, even going so far as to reveal his unhappy past. Anne wondered what had driven him to such ruin. Yet she knew she would not ask unless he chose to confide it.

Breakfast proceeded smoothly.

After the meal, Mr. Tyler said, "I fancy a walk about the estate. I wonder if anyone would be willing to show me the stables and grounds."

"I could," said Jeremy eagerly. "I would love to do it. May I, Anne?"

Despite Lord Westerfield's assurances, Anne still felt a nagging worry over Jeremy. Yet, some of what he had said was true. She did not want to make Jeremy a prisoner in the house.

She turned to her brother and said, "Perhaps we shall both show Mr. Tyler around. You go and tell Betsy to fetch my bonnet."

When Jeremy had hurried to comply, Anne turned to Mr. Tyler. "I do not wish to see danger where there is none. However, a servant girl, Polly, told me she heard that Jeremy was in danger. She said someone hired his tutor to harm him and I do not know why. Perhaps it is not true, but I am worried nonetheless."

To her surprise, Mr. Tyler's face paled as he leaned towards her. "Do you know who did the hiring?"

"No. But Polly said he killed Jeremy's tutor in a quarrel. Perhaps, afterward, the killer went away."

Mr. Tyler shook his head. "I would not count on it. Have you noticed anyone new in the village?"

Anne thought. "No."

Then a sudden memory struck her. "Our 'ostler hired a new man for the stable. He has been driving us around lately."

Mr. Tyler's forehead puckered into a frown. "I think that I should meet this new man."

"Why is that? Is something amiss?"

"Probably not. Yet, it pays to be careful regarding the safety of your brother."

"Then you believe it may be true that a man hired and murdered our tutor?"

"Possibly. I think we should check it out."

"How will we know if it is true? Polly did not even see the man. It was dark and his face was hidden."

"I have met such men before. And, as I am a good judge of character, I think I shall learn something from meeting him."

"Then let us go straight away. I want to know if my brother is in danger."

Jeremy came running back with her bonnet. Anne set it on her head and tied the ribands under her chin. Then the three of them set off for the stables.

Anne felt her apprehension rise as they proceeded along the path. The sharp tang of horseflesh and manure drifted on the breeze, directing Mr. Tyler toward the stables. She wondered if Mr. Tyler would suspect the young driver of foul play. If so, she could not trust her judgment, for she had never noticed anything suspicious about the young man.

They reached the brick exterior of the stables. Bales of amber hay lay stacked beside the open double doors. Horses nickered inside their stalls. Anne saw their new hire, grooming the bay mare that had been Grandfather's favorite when he was able to ride.

She stepped into the interior of the stable. It was cooler and dimmer than the bright summer day. As they paused, the red-cheeked boy turned in surprise, nearly dropping the curry comb.

Anne studied him. He was slim of build and had gentle brown eyes that reminded her of her horse. Surely he could not be a killer. But then, how did she know?

Jeremy began to pet the horse while Mr. Tyler greeted the young groom. "Good-morning. What is your name, my boy?"

"Pete, sir. I am sorry. I did not hear you come in. Do you require a carriage?"

"No, though I may wish to go for a ride later in the afternoon."

Pete bent to pick up the comb. "I shall have a horse ready if you will tell me which you would choose."

"This one looks like a beauty," Mr. Tyler observed.

Anne watched his face for any sign that he found a reason to mistrust Pete. So far, he showed no sign of suspecting ill of the boy. He had relaxed visibly from the tension he displayed after breakfast.

"This is Grandfather's horse. At least he used to be," Jeremy explained wistfully.

"Your grandfather was a good judge of horses," said Mr. Tyler.

He bent down to Jeremy and said, "Would you mind if I rode him?"

Jeremy shook his head. "Grandfather would want him to be ridden."

"Then I shall be honored to do so."

Again, Anne was warmed by Mr. Tyler's concern for Jeremy's feelings.

"I shall go and see my pony," Jeremy said as he trudged away along the rows of stalls.

"Shall you be riding also, miss?" Pete asked.

"No. I shall be keeping an eye on my brother."

Pete stood attentively awaiting further requests.

Anne, weary of the suspense, blurted her questions. "Who hired you, Pete, and how well did you know my brother's tutor, Mr. Ames?"

Pete's dark eyes widened in his thin tanned face. "The 'ostler hired me, miss. I did not know Mr. Ames well at all. I saddled horses for him a few times is all."

Mr. Tyler put a hand on Anne's arm. "It is all right, my dear. Pete is telling the truth."

He turned to the boy and said, "Did you ever see anyone else come to meet with Mr. Ames, someone you did not know?"

"No, sir. I know everyone who has come in here the last few weeks. And Mr. Ames always rode off alone."

"Thank you, Pete. You are doing a fine job on this horse. We shall not detain you any longer from your work. I will tour the stable and come back later for a ride."

"Yes, sir. He will be ready, sir."

Pete patted the bay's sleek neck.

Mr. Tyler strode along the aisle, peering at the stalls. Anne hurried to walk alongside. "You do not think the boy is a danger to my brother?"

"No. He is no danger to anyone, except himself if he drops more than a curry comb onto his foot."

Anne frowned. "How can you be sure?"

He paused before they reached Jeremy, who was in the stall with his pony. Mr. Tyler smiled patiently and said, "Let us think this out. What would a groom have to gain by harming your brother? Nothing. He stands to obtain nothing at all."

Anne thought over his logic. "I suppose you are right. Yet, I still wonder who killed Mr. Ames."

"Perhaps a highwayman."

Anne nodded, feeling a bit comforted.

"What worried, me, "Mr. Tyler explained, "was the possibility that this young man was not truly a groom, but a gentleman posing as such. Such an unsavory sort might think of a way to kidnap your brother for ransom. But this young groom has the calloused hands and tanned features that proclaim him to be who he says he is."

"Well, that is a relief. Lord Westerfield assures me that if there was a danger, the perpetrator has probably left town by now."

"Let us hope he is correct. Nonetheless, I shall keep my eyes open."

"Thank you. You have been very kind not to dismiss my fears. It is hard sometimes to be alone in the responsibility for my brother."

"Then I shall be your ally and hope that my friendship gives you comfort."

"It already has. I believe you have won Jeremy over also."

A sad smile rested on Mr. Tyler's lips as he studied Jeremy petting his pony. "He is a fine boy. I am sure your parents were proud of him."

"They died when Jeremy was very young. He has difficulty remembering them. As you can tell, he grew very close to Grandfather."

Mr. Tyler looked away, an odd expression in his eyes. Then, in a murmur, he said, "A child can be a blessing...in the right circumstances."

Jeremy popped up behind the open top of the stable door and said, "Do you want to see Toby? Grandfather bought him for me when I first came here. He taught me how to ride him."

Mr. Tyler reached across and stroked the pony's mane.

"Perhaps you and I might go riding one day."

Jeremy beamed. "Yes. I should like that. Anne will not let me ride now that Grandfather is gone, even if I take a groom."

"Your sister loves you very much. You must remember that."

Jeremy sighed. "I know."

Anne opened the stall door. "Come, Jeremy. We promised to show Mr. Tyler about."

They walked the grounds. All the while, Mr. Tyler admired the sprawling old oaks, the lush and verdant grasses, and the view of the tenant homes from atop a small rise. They ended at the fish pond where Jeremy proudly pointed out the various fish. For his part, Mr. Tyler could not have been a more gracious admirer of the well-fed occupants of the pond.

They started the walk back, speaking about a minor improvement Mr. Tyler wished to make in a bushy overgrown corner of the park. Engrossed in conversation, Anne did not see the tall dark-haired man who trod toward them until Jeremy let out a cry of greeting.

"Lord Westerfield. I hoped you would come soon."

Westerfield smiled. "And here I am."

He bowed at the group, giving Anne a searching look as he straightened. "I have come to offer a carriage to collect anyone who wants to go on the hunt tomorrow. Then, your man will not have to wait the day at my estate if he should be needed here."

Tearing his gaze away from Anne, he told Mr. Tyler, "I trust that you have been able to rest after your journey."

"Indeed. I have had a most refreshing night and a wonderful morning with Anne and Jeremy, walking the grounds. I must say that I am pleased with what I have seen. I plan to ride about this afternoon and see more of the tenant land. But I should love a hunt on the morrow. Pheasant, is it?"

"Yes. I own a patch of thick woods that they are fond of. I think we shall have good luck."

"And I shall go and see what is done with the dogs," said Jeremy, obviously delighted with the plans.

Westerfield raised his brows as he looked at Anne. "I need to speak to your sister on that matter. I believe she had some concerns. And I do not want to go against her wishes."

Jeremy stopped in his tracks and turned to Anne in distress. "Oh, do not change your mind, Anne, please. You already said I might go."

"Hush now, Jeremy. I am not changing my mind. You may still go."

Jeremy beamed. "Thank you, Anne. Would you all like to see the secret door I found that leads into the kitchen? I found it ever so long ago and quite by accident. There are stairs filled with cobwebs that go up to a hidden door in Grandfather's room."

"How fascinating," said Mr. Tyler. "Did your Grandfather know about it?"

"Oh, yes. He said it had been there for ages. He said I had very good eyes for finding the door to the kitchen. It is covered by bushes and ever so hard to find."

"Indeed, I would like to see it," said Mr. Tyler.

Anne shivered. "You have already shown it to me. It is dark and damp and not very nice."

"Lord Westerfield has not seen it," Jeremy said.

Westerfield smiled at Jeremy. "You go and show it to Mr. Tyler. I want to talk to your sister. I will see the secret passage another time."

"All right."

He took Mr. Tyler's hand. "Come this way, Mr. Tyler. The way up is dark, but you may hold my hand. I will not let you stumble."

Mr. Tyler looked down at the boy. His smile was poignant. "Thank you, Jeremy."

When they were out of hearing, Anne said, "I believe Mr. Tyler and Jeremy are becoming good friends."

Westerfield nodded. "It is easy to like a boy who is so generous with his friendship."

Anne felt her eyes mist as she watched the small figure walk off with Mr. Tyler. "He misses Grandfather. They had a special bond. You and Mr. Tyler have helped him forget his loss."

He stopped under a spreading oak and asked softly, "And who will help you forget your loss?"

For a moment, her tears threatened to spill over. Then, she drew her small shoulders erect and said, "Loss is a part of life. For Jeremy's sake, I must look to the future."

"And what will you do when Jeremy is grown and no longer needs to be looked after? Who will you look after then?"

Anne frowned. A mix of confusing emotions swirled within her. Causing most of her discomposure was the fact that Lord Westerfield was standing close, too close for her to think clearly. The late morning breeze carried the scent of his cologne. His tall body blocked the light of the sun.

Before she could speak, he said, "I paced the floor all evening, feeling miserable about our quarrel. I had no right to criticize how you raise your brother. I know it must be very hard for you."

Anne shook her head. "You need not apologize. Perhaps I did let my imagination run away a bit. I do not want to imprison my brother, nor do I want to make him weak and fearful. I want him to grow up with the same experiences as other boys. I want him to raise a puppy. And I want him to go hunting with you."

Westerfield took her hands and raised them to his lips. "I know you do. And as long as it is in my power, I will never let any harm come to you or to anyone you love. I would protect Jeremy with my life if necessary."

Anne wiped a tear from her eye. "I know. I am sure he will always be safe with you. I am afraid I am a bit prone to worry."

Westerfield smiled and ran a finger along her cheek. "I was going to apologize to you for implying that you worry too much."

She met his dark eyes with a gaze of deep ocean blue. "In that case, I should apologize to you for implying that you worry too little."

"Perhaps we might simply accept each other as we are. Do you think you could accept me, Anne, perhaps even care for me a little?"

Anne felt her pulse race along with her thoughts. Should she admit that she had found him enthralling the first time they met? Not only was he handsome, but he was also kind and thoughtful. Had he not known that a puppy was just what Jeremy had needed to cheer him from his gloom?

And his presence now was just what she needed to cheer her. Had she not suffered just as he had from their quarrel? She had been in misery, wondering if he would cease to call upon her.

She studied the huge gnarled tree root as she formed a reply. Feeling too bashful to meet his eyes, she kept hers glued to the ground as she replied, "I could care for you...more than a little, perhaps."

He raised her chin and stared deeply into her eyes. "You do not know how happy that makes me. I cannot imagine anything more wonderful than spending time with you. The thought that I might have lost you filled me with dread and remorse."

Anne felt as though she had awakened from a bad dream to find that everything was, in fact, all right. She would gladly put their quarrel behind them if that would restore the easy rapport they had shared.

Not wanting the moment to end, she gazed into his eyes, feeling as though she could melt into their warm depths.

He held onto her hands as though he felt equally reluctant to part. Suddenly she had an idea that might prolong his visit.

CHAPTER EIGHT

. . ✿ . .

ANNE SMILED UP AT WESTERFIELD. "I should be pleased if you would stay on until lunch and we might have a picnic. Of course, I shall understand if you have other plans."

He smiled back at her. "I have no other plans. And if I did, I should promptly break them to spend the time with you."

"I shall tell Cook to make up a picnic for us. I cannot tell you how relieved I am to have our difference behind us. I hope that we shall never quarrel again."

Westerfield grinned as he put his arm around her. "That would take all the spice out of life. What good are things without a good quarrel now and then?"

"Pleasant, I should say."

He squeezed her gently and kissed the top of her nose. "I should not like to quarrel with you often, you understand."

They walked together to the house, where Westerfield waited in the library while Anne scurried to request that Cook make up a picnic. When she returned, she found that Mr. Tyler and Jeremy had joined Lord Westerfield. Stamping down the disappointment of losing his undivided attention, she reminded herself that they would soon go on their outing together.

She bided her time while Lord Westerfield and Mr. Tyler discussed the merits of various firearms. She let her thoughts wander to Mariah and her marriage. She wondered if Mariah was happy. She had certainly seemed so when Anne had come upon her and Mr. Fletcher.

After a while, Mr. Tyler brought the conversation round to the subject of lunch. "I am sure I speak for all of us when I request that you join us," he told Westerfield.

Westerfield nodded obligingly. "I thank you for the invitation. I would gladly join your table were it not for the fact that a charming young woman has invited me on a picnic."

Mr. Tyler pulled his chin and pretended to be flummoxed. "Do I know her?"

"Indeed you do, sir, for she is sitting prettily in our midst."

Anne's cheeks flushed pink as Mr. Tyler beamed at her and said, "I can think of no better company on a picnic than our Anne."

"You are both too kind. I do not pretend to be the best of company. I fear, at times, I may be quite dull."

At that, Westerfield let out a chuckle that caused her to blush even more furiously. He shook his head and said, "You, Miss Tyler, are never dull. You never cease to surprise me with your candid views and unassuming ways. I assure you that I treasure them and would never wish for you to change a bit."

Jeremy spoke up. He was bored by the turn of the conversation. Yet, he had heard one thing that interested him. "Are you going on a picnic? May I please come along?"

Anne felt a surge of distress. As much as she loved Jeremy, she longed for this picnic to be solely to get to know Lord Westerfield better. It would be impossible to speak as they liked with the boy along.

Mr. Tyler spoke up quickly. "Why, Jeremy, I had thought you would have lunch with me. If you go off on a picnic, I shall be left alone."

Jeremy was not discouraged. "We could all go."

There was a moment of awkward silence while Jeremy awaited Anne's answer. To be polite, she knew that she had no choice except to invite the entire party. Yet before she braced herself to reply, Mr. Tyler rescued her by saying. "I wanted to see you ride your pony directly after lunch."

He winked at Jeremy. "If we go on a picnic, we shall be stuck all afternoon, sitting around and talking with Lord Westerfield and your sister."

He feigned a whisper and said, "Does that not sound dreadfully dull?"

Jeremy needed no more to be convinced. "Will you really watch me ride my pony?"

Mr. Tyler nodded solemnly. "I should like nothing better. You can show me all of his paces."

Anne felt her conscience prick. "You need not change your plans on account of us. I know you were planning to ride over to the tenanted property today."

Mr. Tyler shook his head. "I can do that any day."

He slapped his thigh. "Today is the day I see Jeremy ride his pony."

Anne smiled her thanks just as Polly came to announce lunch for Jeremy and Mr. Tyler.

"You take care on that pony. No showing off," Anne told Jeremy.

"I shan't."

"I shall see that he is careful," Mr. Tyler promised.

Westerfield took her arm and guided her gently toward the basket that Polly held for them. She realized it was his subtle way of telling her that she was being overprotective again. Instead of taking offense, she allowed him to steer her away.

He took the basket and walked beside her out the open French doors and into the gentle sunlight that was tempered by flocks of lazy clouds that drifted like fleece across the sky.

"I hope it shall not rain," she said.

"Oh, it will not rain."

She gave him a quizzical glance. "How can you be so sure?"

"I am looking forward to our picnic too much to abide any rain."

"And the weather will do as you require?"

He grinned. "The weather will do just as it pleases. I only hope that it pleases me."

She laughed. "Then I need not accuse you of arrogance, for indeed I have seen no hint of that. It is one of the things I like the most about you."

"That is a compliment coming from such a fair-minded person like you."

Anne smiled up at him. "If we go on like this, we shall turn each other's heads and both become insufferable."

"Then, we shall drive everyone else away and be left with only our own company. I could deal quite happily with that."

"You might be sorry for that, in time."

"Then we should improve ourselves with useful criticism. What would you have me change about myself besides meddling in business that is not my own."

Anne thought over his question as they strolled across the lawn to the park on the west side of the house. He set the picnic basket under a shady oak that was home to a squirrel who peered down at them with sharp button eyes. She made a mental note to save over a strawberry or two for his dinner.

"Offhand, I cannot think of any traits that I would condemn. If you give me a bit more time, perhaps I might come up with something."

"How long do you need?"

She smiled mischievously as she shook out their blanket. "Thirty or forty years should do it."

"As a suitor? I do not think I could bear it."

"On that, I can decide much more quickly."

"Perhaps I might help you make up your mind."

He reached out and stroked her cheek. It felt petal soft under his fingers. He traced the outline of her lips, and as they parted, he noted the even whiteness of her teeth. Dare he kiss her? He looked into her eyes and saw the dreaminess of yearning that dwelt in his own heart. He leaned down and claimed her lips in a soft gentle kiss.

As he drew away, he saw her lick her lips as though savoring the feel of their kiss. Her eyes were soft like a doe's and slightly wary. And though he wanted desperately to steal one more kiss, he decided he had better leave that for another time.

He doffed his hat and bowed. "Our lunch awaits, madam. Shall we dine?"

His light-hearted manner broke the spell he had woven between them.

Anne settled herself upon the blanket and began to unpack yeasty white rolls and succulent baked pheasant, cut into thin slices. She pulled out sweet-smelling ripe berries and sharp scented cheese. Wrapped carefully in a cloth, were several sugared cakes, a glass jar of lemonade and two cups.

They sampled the tasty food until appetites sated, they sat back in contentment against the trunk of the tree. Anne could not remember a time when she had felt so content in the company of a gentleman.

She glanced over to see Westerfield pick a leaf of sweet mint and begin to chew so thoughtfully that she said, "I would give a great deal to know your thoughts at this moment."

His scandalously dark eyes fixed her with a gaze so intent that she shivered with anticipation. He had a most discomposing effect upon her. And yet, he charmed her so completely that she longed to see him more often each time they were together.

He discarded the leaf and replied, "My thoughts are no secret. I was thinking what a perfect afternoon it is with perfect company and a wonderful meal. I could hardly be any more content."

"I feel the same."

She looked down bashfully and he found her so enchanting that he captured her small hand and kissed the tips of her fingers.

She caught her lip between her teeth to keep herself from being swept away by the senses he evoked. His lips were warm and moist. They left each finger tingling when he moved to the next, paying exquisite attention to each dainty tip.

At last. he brought her hands to rest against his cheeks. The short stubble of his beard bristled beneath her fingers, reminding her of the masculine scent of his cologne when they had kissed. A part of her longed for him to kiss her again and she knew that, should he do so, she would not resist. Yet later, when she regained her senses, she would chastise herself for behaving in so undisciplined a manner.

He drew her hands together and kissed her palms. Then, releasing her hands he said, "Perhaps we should take a turn about the park. I could use the exercise after indulging in such gluttonous eating. My horse shall refuse to carry me home and I will not blame him one whit."

Anne did not know whether she was more relieved or disappointed. He confused her emotions and troubled her mind. Yet she knew she was as powerless as a grain of sand against the sea in the attraction she felt for Lord Westerfield. She would simply have to ride the tide and see where it took her.

They strolled the small park, stopping to smell wild roses and the jasmine that grew near the wild hedge of hawthorn that separated the park from the thicker undergrowth of a small forest of birch.

They were headed back, following the hedge toward the picnic tree, when a gentle rustling of the bushes caused Anne to drawback. She stifled a screech when a nose poked out from beneath the brush.

As Westerfield knelt to observe the creature, it began a frantic struggle that shook the bushes. He drew on his gloves and began to separate the hedge. Two long velvety ears popped out along with two brown eyes wild with fright.

"There now. Rest easy. I am only trying to free you," he said soothingly.

Anne knelt beside him, relieved to see that it was only a dear little rabbit trapped among the thorns. The creature struggled in fits and spurts and then relaxed completely, feigning demise.

At last, Westerfield untangled the sharp thorns from the fluff of fur and spread the branches so that the rabbit might escape. It sat quite still for a moment, as though frozen with fright, and then, with a frantic burst of speed, it dashed from its prison and disappeared into a burrow on the far side of the park.

Anne felt touched by Westerfield's kindness in rescuing such a small helpless creature. His sympathy for the poor rabbit told her much more than mere words could ever have said about his character.

"That was a thoughtful thing to do."

"I am only happy that we heard the unhappy creature. It would have starved or been found by a dog soon enough."

"And yet they are hunted by those very dogs, are they not?"

"Indeed. But I believe they should be given a sporting chance to run. I know I should not like to meet my end trapped in my own jacket."

"Nor should I," Anne agreed.

Westerfield picked up the picnic basket, which was light now after being emptied. They walked back to the house, absorbed in their thoughts. A maid took the basket when they reached the door to the kitchen.

"Will you come along tomorrow for the hunt?" Westerfield asked.

Anne frowned a bit. "I have never been on a hunt. Watching the killing of birds does not appeal to me. However, I do wish to keep an eye on Jeremy. So, yes, I shall come."

Westerfield grinned. "Then I will look forward to it all the more."

"When should we arrive?"

"Let us say at ten o'clock. Then, you can all stay on to lunch. That will please Father."

Anne nodded. "He is a most gracious gentleman."

"He has taken quite a liking to you. He will never forgive me if I do not manage to bring you to Westerfield Manor."

Anne felt her heart begin to race. Was he bordering on a proposal? Was she ready? What about Jeremy?

Leaving the comment to rest, Westerfield changed the subject. "The picnic was a treat. Perhaps you would allow me to escort you to the ball being given in honor of the newly married Mr. and Mrs. Fletcher."

Anne's cheeks warmed at the possibility of being cut from the guest list. "Have you an invitation?"

"Not yet. But I have heard rumors of it."

"I do not know if I shall be invited. Mariah and I have had a bit of a rift."

Westerfield took her hand. "If you are not welcome, then I shall not go either. We shall go into the village and have our supper. I think I should prefer it."

Anne smiled at his earnest declaration. "I shall let you know if I receive an invitation. If not, I shall take you up on having supper."

He took her hand and bestowed a kiss. "I should be going now. You will not forget your promise to come tomorrow?"

"I will not forget."

He released her hand and tipped his hat. "Then I shall see you on the morrow."

He crunched along the back garden path to the front of the house where his mount waited. Anne stood in the garden. Her emotions were in a whirl. He had come close to saying that he wished to marry her and take her to Westerfield Manor. What would she have said? Her heart told her she would have agreed, leaving her mind to work out the details.

She found herself smiling and humming as she went about her afternoon. She did not even get upset when Jeremy reluctantly admitted to falling off the pony while attempting a jump.

"Perhaps that will teach you to be more careful," Anne said without looking up from embroidering roses onto a pillow.

Jeremy stared at her a moment in surprise before he shrugged and walked away.

The next morning dawned with gray and overcast skies that threatened to put a chill into the air. Anne opened her window and studied the clouds that hung like battleships in a misty sea. Moisture on the outside of her windowsill told her that it had drizzled overnight. If they were not rained out for the hunt, she must remember to bring along a warm woolen shawl.

As she breakfasted in her room, an impatient rapping at her door told her Jeremy was eager to be off. She bid him come in and noticed that he had neither combed his hair nor properly buttoned his shirt. He had no patience when it came to a choice between personal grooming and going on an outing.

"Are you not ready, Anne? It must be nearly time to go."

"Not for over an hour, dear. Have you had your breakfast?"

"Yes. Very early. Betsy brought it in."

"Well, you will have to amuse yourself while I finish my breakfast and dress. Have you seen Mr. Tyler?"

"No. But I know he is having breakfast because I saw Betsy take in his tray."

"I shall have to conference with him regarding the weather. I hope it does not preclude our outing."

Jeremy scowled. "It had better not. I shall go out and look at the clouds."

Anne smiled. "Jeremy, you are no more in control of the weather than is Lord Westerfield."

"I know. But I do hope it does not storm."

"Comb your hair and button your shirt correctly. Then you may go out if you wear a jacket."

"All right. But we shall go. I know we shall."

After Anne finished her breakfast, Betsy helped her dress in a sensible cotton gown. She donned black button boots instead of slippers. If she were going to hike the woods, she intended to dress for the occasion.

She left her room just as Mr. Tyler was emerging from his chamber. It seemed he had little concern regarding the weather. "It is sure to clear up later in the morning. It always does on days such as this."

So taking his word, the party set out in the carriage for Westerfield Manor. To prove Mr. Tyler correct, the weather began to clear before they reached the fork in the road. As they crossed onto the lane leading to the manor, Mariah's carriage approached from the other direction. Anne had her driver slow so that she might greet Mariah. Her effort was in vain, as Mariah turned her head away and clattered past without any greeting.

Anne sighed. Perhaps she should assume the friendship was ended and get on with her life. After all, Mariah had pointed out that she was a married woman while Anne was still single. The thought of marriage made a tingle run through her spine that made her forget all about Mariah. She would see the lord today. Would he make any further hints toward a declaration in form? The possibility kept her in a constant state of the jitters. Yet it was pleasant anticipation that made her look forward to his visit.

They arrived at the manor to find Lord Westerfield waiting outside. He grinned broadly as they pulled to a stop. He helped Anne from the carriage and then lifted Jeremy down. When Mr. Tyler joined them, Lord Westerfield greeted his guests with a bow.

"Welcome to Westerfield Manor. I trust that you had a pleasant journey."

"Yes. Fortunately, it is not far. I do not believe young Jeremy could have stood a longer trip," said Mr. Tyler.

Anne had a more serious concern. "We passed Mariah Fletcher on the way into the estate."

Lord Westerfield shifted about, looking discomfited. "Yes, she delivered the invitation to the ball. Perhaps she is stopping at your house next."

"Possibly," Anne agreed, though she did not believe it was true.

Their attention shifted as one of the stable hands brought the dogs round. They pulled at their chains in eagerness to begin the hunt. Yet a stern command from Lord Westerfield had them sitting obediently at his feet.

He passed a gun to Mr. Tyler and grinned down at Jeremy. "Now we shall show you how this is done."

"May I see my puppy?"

"You will have plenty of time to visit your puppy after lunch. Now, it is time to hunt."

Anne wrapped her shawl about her and trod with the men toward the forest that lay on the east side of the estate. It consisted of a thick copse of trees that thinned at the edges into the meadow they now crossed.

She put her hand on Jeremy's shoulder and said, "You are not to wander away. I shall not have you getting lost or mistaken for game and shot."

Westerfield glanced down at the boy. "You will stay right with us and not worry your sister, will you not?"

Jeremy nodded. "I want to watch what you do."

They entered the woods and sent the dogs rummaging into the bushes to flush out the birds. Several quail rose at once from one of the bushes. The dogs froze as the men aimed into the sky and one of the birds fell. Jeremy jumped with excitement as the dogs set off to retrieve it.

"My dog can learn to do that. I know he can."

"Of course," said Westerfield. "But he will need training."

They repeated the process several times, yet were not always successful. Anne doubted that Mr. Tyler had hit a bird at all. Yet, his enthusiasm made up for his lack of skill. He aimed shot after shot, prompted along by Westerfield's cheerful encouragement.

The grooms kept up their end of the job by pouring flask after flask of black powder into the barrels and carefully tamping it down. And though Anne had never cared for guns, she admired the efficient competency of the three groomsmen. It seemed they were always ready to hand over a fresh gun as soon as it was required.

By the time they had a half-dozen birds, it had begun to drizzle. The men were engrossed in their pursuit and did not seem to notice. Anne pulled her shawl more closely about her to help stop her shivers.

She was relieved when Westerfield tied a dozen birds on a string to be carried back by the groomsmen. Her hair curled in damp ringlets beneath her bonnet. Her shawl felt clammy beneath her hands. Soon she would be soaked through.

Everyone was admiring the bounty when a shot broke the hush of the woods, sending sparrows and larks fleeing from their treetop roosts.

They turned as one to see who had fired the shot. The woods seemed deserted except for their small party. Lord Westerfield made a quick assessment of their surroundings, his sharp eyes missing nothing.

When he spotted no one, he asked, "Did anyone see who fired that shot?"

They all shook their heads.

The shot had given Anne quite a start. She put her arms around Jeremy and glanced anxiously about. When he wriggled to get free, she held him more tightly and asked, "Was someone firing at us?"

Finishing his perusal of the forest around them, Westerfield said, "I believe it must have been a stray shot from a poacher. I shall send my men to investigate. My tenants have my permission to hunt here, but they are to let me know first."

Anne clutched Jeremy's shoulder, ready to march him from the woods. "If someone is hunting, then we should not be here."

Mr. Tyler gave a nervous glance about. "You are right, dear. It is not safe."

Westerfield nodded. "Shall we go back to the house? The weather has turned unkind and you all must be cold."

Anne could feel her knees trembling as they walked toward the edge of the woods. All the while, trees bent over them like haughty sentries who would prevent their escape. The musty scent of damp earth and tall trees lost its allure.

When they reached the edge of the woods, Anne breathed a little easier. Here, they would not be mistaken for prey. She was thankful that no one had been injured, as she had endured enough loss of those she loved. If she had her way, none of her men would go hunting. Not if, there was the possibility of having them catch a stray bullet.

Lord Westerfield looked down into her face and said, "I am sorry you were frightened. I cannot think who might have been trespassing. My tenants are very good about asking permission to hunt."

Mr. Tyler patted her shoulder. "We are all unharmed and can be grateful for that. I say we go on about the day and forget all about it."

Lord Westerfield shook his head. "I shall not forget it until I have sent out my men. If they find someone, I shall give him a tongue-lashing for neglecting to obtain my permission."

Anne watched Jeremy run ahead. "I am vastly relieved that no one was injured. It may be a while before Jeremy and I go hunting again."

"I entirely understand," said the lord.

They left off the quail and freshened themselves for lunch. The elder lord was awaiting them at a long dining table that gleamed like glass and smelled of polish. He greeted them all genially and asked about the hunt. When told of the mishap, he became agitated.

"We must order men out to the woods. We cannot allow this sort of thing to happen."

"Calm yourself, Father. I have already sent the men. If anyone is skulking around, they will find them."

Thus, assured, the elder lord took pleasure in presiding over his table. When they were finished with the meal, a servant was sent to fetch the pup and Jeremy was excused to the kitchen to play with his dog while the adults withdrew to the parlor to visit.

When at last it grew late in the afternoon, Mr. Tyler said, "As much as I have enjoyed your hospitality, I fear we must be off. I have a great deal of paperwork to make sense of regarding the estate."

The elder lord sent a servant to fetch Jeremy and they bid their host good-bye. Young Lord Westerfield saw them to the carriage.

"I shall look forward to another outing," he said.

Though he addressed both of them, his eyes were on Anne.

"It was a most pleasant visit," she said.

Jeremy joined them as they mounted the carriage.

As they drove away, Lord Westerfield waved until they were out of sight.

They arrived home just in time to rest awhile before supper. Anne was on her way up the stairs when a thought struck her.

"Betsy, did I receive any mail today?"

"Yes, miss. Mrs. Fletcher brought something by for you."

Anne descended to the foot of the stairs where Mr. Tyler stood, purveying the letters on the silver salver. He handed her the note from Mariah. And, to her surprise, she found that she had indeed been invited to the ball. She smiled to herself thinking that it would be a pleasure to attend with Lord Westerfield, even if Mariah was mad at her.

She glanced up to see Mr. Tyler scanning a note delivered to him. His face had drained of color. As he sagged against the banister, Anne forgot all about the ball and reached out to steady him, knowing he must have had dreadful news.

CHAPTER NINE

. . ❧ . .

"I SEE THAT SOMETHING has disturbed you. Please, you must rest yourself," Anne said.

Mr. Tyler allowed her to help him into the parlor, where he sank into a plush chair. His face looked drawn as he ran his hand down his chin. Anne stood watching him and wondered what to do.

"May I get you anything? A little wine, perhaps? You look very ill indeed."

He shook his head. "I had hoped that he had gone away and left me to live in peace. But it is not to be. I shall never be rid of him as long as I am alive. And he will never forgive me for not accepting him as my son."

Anne sank into the chair beside him. "Would you like to tell me what has happened?"

"It is a sordid story. One I should have told you sooner. However, I thought that by refusing him, he would drop the matter. He came to me for money in London. When he found that I had none and that your Grandfather had died, he gave me an ultimatum. I never thought that even he could be that evil. I told him to get out of my sight and that I hoped to never see him again."

"Will you tell me the ultimatum? Perhaps I can help," Anne said.

"I am embarrassed I did not tell you before since it concerns your brother."

"Jeremy?"

Anne felt her pulse begin to pound. She had the ominous feeling that she was not going to like what he might say. And yet, if it concerned Jeremy, she was determined to know."

Mr. Tyler sighed. "I should start at the beginning. And it is not a pleasant tale for me to tell. Before my "son" was born, if indeed he is my son, I discovered that my wife was unfaithful to me. Yet she insisted that he was mine. After he was born, she left the babe with me and ran off with her lover. When the boy was old enough, I sent him away to boarding school and rarely saw him."

Anne frowned. "That is a shocking tale. No wonder you did not admit to him. It must have been very hard for you. But how does it involve Jeremy?"

"Well you see, my wife returned to me a few years later. It seems that her lover had deserted her and she wished me to take her back. I could not abide the idea and refused. A few days later, she committed suicide by plunging from the top of my roof. The boy blames me for his mother's death. Despite her faults, she did come to see him occasionally at the boarding school."

A bird shrieked as it flew past the open window. Anne jumped at the sound. Every nerve in her body was on edge as she waited to learn how all of this would affect Jeremy.

"After Lora's death, I became addicted to too much drink and lost my home and business. This went on for several years. When my son, if he is my son, came to see me a few months ago, I had just thrown off my penchant for alcohol, but I still had no money. He told me I owed him some sort of inheritance. With your grandfather dead, he knew I would become the guardian of his estate. And as my only son, it would eventually fall into his hands if Jeremy were out of the way."

Anne shook her head. "That is all true."

Mr. Tyler wiped his forehead with his kerchief. "My *son* is an evil creature, thinking that others think in the same ill way as him. He told me that I must find a way to dispose of your brother when I came here."

Anne felt incredulous. "He would have a child killed to inherit a house?"

Mr. Tyler nodded. "Exactly true, as ridiculous as it sounds. Of course, I told him I would have nothing to do with such a scheme. He became enraged and told me I owed it to him. When I still refused, he stomped away and I thought that was the end of the matter."

Anne shivered as she stared at the letter he clutched loosely in his hand. "Then what has he said in the letter?"

"He said the shot in the forest was a warning. I have one last chance to do as he requests."

"And if you do not?"

"He does not say."

Mr. Tyler took her hand and said earnestly, "I wonder if you should not send your brother away from here. Perhaps he should go to a boarding school and we would not tell anyone where he had gone. I am very fond of Jeremy and do not believe I could stand it if he were harmed."

Anne looked into the watery blue of Mr. Tyler's eyes and said, "I do not believe I can send Jeremy away. I would not feel he was safe. What if he was somehow found out? I would not even be there to help him."

Mr. Tyler sighed. His drawn face held no sign of its usual good humor. "I suppose you are right. And yet, I regret what has happened. You can understand why I was so concerned when you told me you had a new groom. I would not put it past my son to pose as a groom to do his mischief. Yet, when I saw that he was not, and there was no one new in town, I felt as though I might relax a bit."

Anne gave his hand a gentle squeeze. "I thank you for telling me all of this. I know that it was painful for you."

"It was. But my fear for Jeremy was much stronger."

"Do not worry. I shall keep Jeremy in the house until your son is found out."

"Perhaps Lord Westerfield's men located him in the woods. I shall ride over tomorrow and see what he has discovered."

Anne brightened a little. "Yes. Perhaps he was found and has been detained. Once you identify him, we will know our enemy. And mayhaps he could be jailed on your testimony."

"I believe you are right. And once he is found out, all will be well. I believe I shall go to my room now and call for brandy. My nerves are quite shaken after this shock."

Anne smiled at him fondly. "You should go and rest. I will talk with Jeremy and explain that he must stay in the house for a few days."

"I think that is a wise idea."

Mr. Tyler walked away, hunched by the burden he carried.

Anne called for Betsy.

"Please find Master Jeremy. I wish to speak to him."

Betsy curtsied and went away to comply.

The minutes ticked by. Anne sat in solitude and listened for Jeremy's footsteps. Yet the only sound she heard was the window curtains rustling in the gentle breeze and the muffled clang of pans in the kitchen.

She became restless. What could be taking so long?

At last, Betsy returned. She reported in a solemn tone that the young master was not in the house. Should she send Polly out to the gardens to look for him?

Anne sprang to her feet. "No, thank you, Betsy. I think I know where he has gone. I shall look for him myself."

"Very well, miss."

Not pausing for her bonnet, Anne fairly flew out the door and down the garden path. She had one purpose in mind. And that was to find her brother before Mr. Tyler's son came upon him.

She ran full speed toward the pond, praying all the while that she would find him there unharmed. After all, no one could have known that he would leave the house. Unless...the house was being watched.

A burning stitch in her side begged her to stop and rest. She ignored it and pressed on, feeling as though her lungs would burst.

At last, she saw his dark hair as he knelt beside the pond. She allowed herself to slow to a trot, so relieved to find Jeremy unharmed that tears blurred her vision. She threw herself beside him and gasped. "Why did you not tell someone that you were going out?"

Jeremy stared at her in surprise. "I never thought to. You have never minded me coming here before."

Anne took a deep breath to calm herself. "You are right, of course. But we must go back now. There is something I would speak to you about."

Her worried eyes and serious tone made Jeremy suspicious. "Did I do something wrong?"

"No, dear, not you. But someone else wishes to do you harm and we must make sure that he does not get a chance."

"Who is it?"

"Mr. Tyler's son. Now come with me to the house and I will tell you a little more about it."

Anne felt as though every nerve in her body was intently alive as she escorted Jeremy back to the house. She glanced behind her, shivering at the thought that they made perfect targets. It was only when they entered the house and shut the door that she finally began to relax.

She pulled Jeremy into the parlor and sat down for a serious talk.

"Mr. Tyler has a son. He is not a very nice man and wants to do us harm. So, we must stay in the house for a few days until he is caught and the danger passes. Do you understand?"

Jeremy frowned. "Yes. But why should he want to hurt us?"

Anne sighed. She had hoped not to tell Jeremy that he was in particular danger.

"You see, dear, he is heir to this estate if you and Mr. Tyler should die. He is an evil man who wishes to get his hands on it any way he can."

The confusion on Jeremy's small face set an ache in her heart.

"I do not even know him," he protested.

"I know. And that is the danger. Will you promise me to stay in the house until it is safe to go out again?"

Jeremy nodded. "I will not like being confined, but I will look at Grandfather's books."

Anne leaned over and kissed his soft cheek. "You are a good boy. You are all the family I have and I love you very much."

He wrapped his arms around her neck and squeezed her. "I love you, too, Anne."

She patted his back and said, "Run along and play upstairs until time for your supper."

She did not see Mr. Tyler again that evening. He took supper in his room and then kept to his chamber. Anne wandered the house until late in the night. She had called the servants together and put them on alert. Nonetheless, the worry that young Mr. Tyler might try to enter while they slept made her too uneasy to retire.

Finally, her loyal Betsy sent her off to bed, proclaiming, "I shall stay awake all night and keep watch. You must get some sleep, miss. You look ready to drop."

Assured by Betsy's determination to keep vigil, Anne gave in and went to bed. Exhaustion overtook her and she dropped immediately into sleep. Her dreams were troubled and she awoke very early in the morning, sure that she had heard a sound. She sprang from her bed and pulled on her wrap.

She hurried down the hall to Jeremy's room and opened the door softly, needing only to see that he was safely asleep. A feeling of horror swept over her to see that, not only was he not asleep, he was not in his bed. She dashed about calling him and checking every corner of the room. Yet, there was no mistaking that he was nowhere to be found.

Running down the stairs, she met Betsy at the bottom. The poor dear lady held an iron, frying skillet in her hand, ready to do battle.

"I heard the commotion and came running. You just tell me where he is."

"I am looking for Jeremy. He is not in his room."

"Not in his room? He could not have got past me. I have been sitting in the hallway all night."

The women flew about the house, calling his name, waking the rest of the servants who dressed quickly and joined in the search.

"He could not have gone out," Anne moaned. "He promised me."

She was feeling near hysterics as they broadened the search, sending servants to the gardens and out to the pond. Though she insisted otherwise, Anne could only assume that Betsy had fallen asleep, allowing someone entrance to the house. However, a thorough check of windows and doors, showed them locked with no sign of forced entry.

She spun on her heel to go back through the kitchen and join the search outside when she nearly collided with Jeremy. He was rubbing his eyes sleepily and staring about.

"I woke up and heard everyone calling me."

Anne clasped him so tightly to her chest that he could hardly breathe. She released him after a moment and said, "How could you frighten me so? I thought you had been taken during the night."

Jeremy wiped at a tear that rolled down her cheek and said, "I am sorry. I woke up in the middle of the night and was frightened. I hid on the secret stairs behind Grandfather's room and fell back asleep. I thought I would wake before anyone worried."

Anne brushed away the rest of her tears. "You cannot imagine how worried I was. But I do think you had a clever idea. Only a few of us know about the stairs, so you would not be easily found."

"Is it time for breakfast?" Jeremy asked. "I am frightfully hungry."

Anne laughed. "If you are hungry, it is time for breakfast."

Mr. Tyler ambled into the hallway, having been waked by having his room checked by the servants. "I took a sleeping potion last night to help me rest. I am afraid it has left me a bit drowsy."

They all went upstairs to dress properly before coming back down for breakfast. There, Anne told Mr. Tyler the whole story.

"And that is why Betsy did not see him," Anne concluded.

He shook his head and muttered how sorry he was to have brought this trouble upon them. "It is a clever hiding spot. Yet, it is too cold and damp to stay there at night. Still, I do not know what lowness my son might stoop to accomplish his purpose. Perhaps a bed could be moved into my room. I shall keep a pistol nearby to protect Jeremy."

Anne shivered. "I suppose that is better than a damp stairway."

As they were concluding breakfast, Polly announced that a visitor had arrived.

Lord Westerfield entered with a bow.

"I was just coming to see you this morning," said Mr. Tyler.

At the mere sight of his strong confident entry, Anne felt her nerves relax. If she were a damsel in distress, he was most surely her knight. And he fit the form so beautifully that she could not help but smile.

"Did you discover the intruder in the woods?" asked Mr. Tyler.

When he replied that he had not, he was told the entire sordid story while Jeremy was sent away to his room.

"What an entirely unfortunate business," he said. "To harm a child is the lowest form of cowardice."

"What shall we do about the ball tomorrow?" Anne asked. "I cannot leave my brother here where he might be attacked."

Westerfield rubbed his chin. "No. I think you dare not. Yet, I have an idea. We will take Jeremy to my father. No one will suspect that he will be there. I will loose the dogs and post a few men to guard the chamber where he may spend the night."

Anne thought it over. "Yes. I believe he would be safer there. I will not worry if he is guarded at your house."

"Good. Then it is settled. The miscreant will be found out in time and we will let no harm come to Jeremy."

They spoke of more pleasant things until Mr. Tyler said that he was still fatigued and begged off for a rest in his room.

Anne invited Westerfield for a walk in the garden. "The roses are in such beautiful bloom and the smell of lilacs so sweet."

They strolled together out to the hedge roses that formed a maze leading to a rectangular bed of daisies swaying in the breeze.

"They remind me of dainty dancers," Anne said.

"Hum. There is a ball tomorrow and I am feeling a bit rusty with dancing," he replied. "Perhaps we should have a practice."

Anne laughed. "Here? There is no music."

He took her in his arms. "Then we shall make our own."

They swirled along the stone path that framed the daisies, moving gracefully as one being. Westerfield felt as though he could hold her small form close to his body forever and breathe the fresh scent of lavender that scented her hair.

He had begun to imagine a future together. He could not even fathom one without her. He had crossed a line from which he could never return. His heart was committed now and would either be shattered or elated. The choice was hers.

When they had danced a while, Lord Westerfield reluctantly explained that he had been on his way to the village on an errand when he had stopped by. "I should be on my way. Father is expecting me back in time for lunch."

"I am happy that you came. I have enjoyed our dance, even without the music."

"Tomorrow we shall dance again." He leaned down and kissed her very gently on the lips. "Let this be a token of my esteem until I see you again."

Anne walked him to his horse and watched him ride away. When he had left, she felt alone again and much too eager for her knight to return.

All the next day, Anne remained in a state of excitement. She occasionally thought about how Mariah might receive her and finally decided that Mariah dare not cut her while she was with Lord Westerfield, who was above both her and her husband in social stature.

Jeremy was nearly as excited as Anne. The idea of spending the night at Westerfield Manor appealed to him immediately. Anne believed that the elder lord reminded him of his beloved grandfather. And it did not hurt that the puppy was there, either.

They were each ready promptly at eight o'clock. Anne had dressed carefully in royal blue silk with an overskirt of blue silk. Tiny silk forget-me-knots edged each of the sleeves. With a high waistline and slightly daring décolletage, it showed her small figure off to advantage.

There was no doubt of Lord Westerfield's approval when he arrived. "However did you choose a dress the same color as your eyes, the finest eyes I have ever seen?"

"I assure you, sir, that it was quite without intent, though I am pleased you approve."

He bowed. "I approve indeed. I shall have the prettiest partner at the ball."

He glanced down at Jeremy. "Do you not agree?"

"Yes. Anne is always the prettiest girl at any party."

Anne laughed. She gave Jeremy's head an affectionate tussle. "And how many parties have you attended?"

He thought a moment and answered honestly, "None."

Nonetheless, Anne was touched by his childish loyalty and loving nature. If he retained the same qualities of character as a man that he possessed as a boy, she would be pleased indeed. She had determined long ago that she would not dishonor the memory of her parents by failing in the rearing of Jeremy. And to her relief, he was proving to be a child with an easy nature to manage.

Lord Westerfield knelt to the boy. "Are you ready to spend the evening with my father? He is looking forward to your company. He has even planned several card games to play when you arrive."

"But I do not know any card games."

"All the better," laughed Westerfield. "He will take great pleasure in teaching you."

They loaded themselves into the carriage and set off. Anne kept strict propriety while in the carriage, though Lord Westerfield insisted upon twirling a lock of her chestnut hair around his finger.

"You have beautiful hair. I like how you have swept it up from your face, leaving ringlets that I may tease."

"Tease them too much and I shall look as though Betsy never touched my hair."

He laughed. "I shall not muss it, I promise, though it is a tempting thought."

When they reached his house, they left Jeremy in the custody of the elder lord. As predicted by his son, he was delighted to see the boy and delighted to have company for the evening. They left them to cake and milk and the learning of a new game.

Anne felt free of her worries as they set out for the Sawyer residence. "I wonder when Mariah and Troy will move to a home of their own."

Westerfield looked thoughtful. "Fletcher does not seem in any hurry to budge from his nest there. Perhaps he has been made too comfortable and is not the sort of chap to move out unless forced to do so."

"Perhaps. He claimed to be looking for a house when I first met him. I am beginning to wonder if he is in earnest about finding one at all."

Westerfield shook his head. "He has not taken me into his confidence. Indeed, I know him very little. But I must admit I have not been impressed by what I have seen."

"Nor have I," Anne agreed.

Anne sucked in a breath when they arrived at the house. Light spilled from every window. A festive trail of luminaries ran from the edge of the drive to the front door. Music drifted to them from the night air that carried the scent of dozens of bouquets of lilacs and roses, mums and carnations.

They were admitted into the foyer to a fairy land of sight and sound. Garlands decorated every mantel and stair rail. The scent of cakes and puddings, roast pork and pies filled the air. On the dance floor, dancers swirled about in a graceful waltz.

Anne smiled up at Lord Westerfield as he took her into his arms and led her with expert ease around the floor. They waltzed past Mariah who was dancing with Troy. Anne was surprised to see that she wore a most unhappy look upon her face. She glanced at Anne and lowered her eyes, yet Anne had already seen the misery in their depths.

Throughout the evening, Anne sent covert glances at Mariah and never saw her smile. Something was wrong. She longed to corner her friend and ask. Yet Mariah had made it plain they were no longer on intimate terms.

They spoke briefly at supper, congratulating Mr. Fletcher on his choice of a bride and wishing them both the best for their future. Mariah received their wishes politely, yet displayed a downcast mood at odds with her usual cheerful enthusiasm. Anne could not mention her worry to Westerfield until they were again alone.

"Perhaps they argued before the ball began. Despite your desire that couples avoid arguments, I do not think it easy to achieve," he said.

She nodded. "Perhaps you are right."

Since there was no reason to arrive home early, they danced until the evening grew quite late and their feet grew sore. Anne felt as though she would fall over from exhaustion by the time they returned to the carriage. Yet, she would not have traded a moment of her evening with Lord Westerfield for any night's rest she might have got.

She allowed him to sit beside her on the ride home. She was resting her head comfortably against his shoulder and feeling pleasantly drowsy when he gently took her hands and said, "My dear Miss Tyler, there is something of the greatest importance that I wish to discuss with you. Will you hear me tonight or are you too weary?"

She sat up, suddenly livened by the tone of his voice. "After what you have just said, I could not stand to wait. I must know what is pressing so heavily upon your mind."

"Then I shall tell you and hope that you are agreeable, for if you are not, I shall be sorely disappointed."

Thus said, Lord Westerfield cleared his throat and spoke.

CHAPTER TEN

HE WATCHED HER FACE as the moon slipped from the clouds and lit her delicate features. Her eyes were twin jewels, glittering with curiosity. Her lips parted slightly in anticipation.

"It can be no surprise to you that I enjoy your company very much and I wish to make it a permanent part of my life. My admiration and affection have deepened to the point that I cannot imagine life without you. So, I am led to confess that I love you and wish to make you my wife. Will you marry me, my lovely Miss Tyler?"

The intensity in his dark eyes sent a shiver down her spine, igniting her senses like a fire sweeping through dry brush. She could not imagine a future without him, for he had captured her heart as surely as she had captured his.

She licked her lips, priming herself for the biggest decision of her life. Casting off her natural inclination for caution, she said, "I return both your affection and admiration. I will marry you, Lord Westerfield."

He clasped her hands to his chest. "You have made me the happiest man alive. Perhaps, when the unfortunate business of Mr. Tyler's son is behind us, we might set a date. With that as an inducement, I shall work tirelessly to solve his identity."

"And I shall be grateful for your help."

"There is nothing I would not do for you."

He pulled her to him and kissed her long and tenderly. Anne melted against him, enjoying the warmth of his lips and the steady beating of his heart. Her cares melted away. She was no longer on her own now that she had Westerfield to help her. It seemed no evil could touch her within the solid protection of his arms.

When they reached her home, they parted reluctantly.

"I am so glad Jeremy is with your father tonight. I shall come for him in the morning."

"When you arrive, my men and I will arm ourselves and see you safely back."

"I would be grateful."

"I would not have it otherwise."

He leaned down for a kiss before he departed. "I will keep a close eye on your brother. He will not come to harm."

"I do not fear for him when he is with you."

He smiled down at her as he ran a finger across her lips. "All will be well, you will see."

He departed and Anne returned to the house, still feeling the touch of his finger upon her lips. All night she dreamed of him. When she awoke, she wondered if she had only dreamed he had proposed. A sense of disappointment filled her until she came fully awake and remembered she had truly ridden home with Lord Westerfield.

She smiled as she drew her feet from beneath the covers and rang for Betsy. She would dress and eat breakfast. After that, she would send for the carriage and go for Jeremy. She was filled with anticipation for the morning. Not only would she see her brother, but she would see Lord Westerfield again and prove to herself that last night had not been a dream.

Betsy appeared promptly with breakfast. She helped Anne dress and smooth her hair into waves that parted in the middle and swept to her shoulder blades. Then, dressing in yellow summer cotton with petite blue flowers, she donned her slippers and ate her breakfast.

The young groom, Pete, drove her out to Westerfield Manor. Anne's thoughts raced ahead. What would it be like to be mistress of the fine old estate? And to think, she had worried about being homeless if Mr. Tyler had not wished her to stay.

She felt sure the elder Lord Westerfield would be pleased to welcome her to his household. And Jeremy could live with them. He had taken to the elderly Lord Westerfield just as he had his grandfather. She only hoped he had not been a bother during the evening.

When she arrived, she was greeted immediately by both her brother and Lord Westerfield. They were on the front lawn beginning to train the puppy.

"Lord Westerfield's father let me keep Duke in my room all night. Was that not a perfectly nice thing to do?" Jeremy enthused.

Westerfield greeted Anne with a smile. "They had a wonderful time. Father talked all morning about how much he enjoyed having the boy in the house. He will be ecstatic when I tell him of our conversation in the carriage."

Anne blushed. "I hope he shall be pleased."

"No doubt of it. He already thinks highly of you and pesters me constantly to have you to tea. Will you stay and have a cup?"

Anne laughed. "How could I turn down such a kind invitation?"

She turned to Jeremy. "Come along, dear. What shall we do with the dog?"

"Lord Westerfield said that I may take him home now."

She raised a brow. "Yes? Well, that is wonderful. But you may not keep him in the house. We shall find a place for him in the stable."

Jeremy sighed. "May I not keep him in my room as I did last night? He was very quiet. If I must stay always indoors, he might keep me company so I am not so lonely."

Thinking of him confined to the house touched Anne's heart and she felt herself relenting. "We shall see. He shall have to be a very good dog and not mess about the house."

"I will keep a very good eye on him," Jeremy promised.

"Well come along for now. We shall decide about the puppy later."

"You may take him in the kitchen for a treat if you like. Tell Cook I said you might," Westerfield suggested.

Jeremy skipped ahead, the puppy at his heels, en route to the kitchen.

Westerfield put his arm around Anne and led her into the house. "I missed you all night and could not wait for you to arrive."

She smiled up at him. "I missed you, too."

They found the elder lord dozing in the drawing-room, a book and a blanket in his lap. He came to life quickly enough when he discovered Anne had arrived. He beamed at her and said, "I suppose I am worn out from the young man's youthful enthusiasm. It did me good, though. It made me feel younger, too."

"I am glad he was not too much bother."

"None at all. I was glad to have him. He may come back any time he likes."

He winked at Anne. "My son has very little time these days to play games and amuse me."

The younger lord settled Anne in a chair and rang for tea. "I have little time because I must spend it persuading this young lady that I am worthy of her attentions. I believe I have succeeded, for she has agreed to become my wife."

Anne would not have believed it possible for the elder lord to smile a broader, more delighted smile.

"I am happy indeed," he crowed. "I have hoped to live to see my son wed and perhaps a grandchild or two. And now that we have Anne, I am more than happy. I am elated. I could find no prettier and sweet-tempered daughter in all the world."

Anne felt overwhelmed by the praise. "I think your estimation does me more credit than due, but I am truly complimented to become your daughter. I believe we shall get on splendidly."

"We must have a party; just a small party, to celebrate. I want news of the engagement to get out to everyone in the county. And we must do it soon so that Anne does not have a chance to change her mind."

Lord Westerfield chuckled. "You possess little confidence in my ability to retain Anne's affection, sir."

The older man shook his head and said in all seriousness, "You cannot take chances when much is at stake."

Anne patted his hand. "Do not worry, sir. I shall not change my mind."

She looked up at the young lord. Her eyes grew misty as she said, "I love your son and he loves me."

"Then I am truly happy for you both. I loved my wife dearly and have never completely recovered from the loss," said the elder lord.

Changing the subject, he asked Anne, "You will get me your guest list soon?"

"I promise that I shall do it this very week."

The tea arrived and was placed on the table.

Anne poured; enjoying the homey duty in what would soon become her drawing-room in her own house. They had a nice long chat as they lingered, enjoying one another's company.

"I understand that you have no female relatives. Who will help you plan your trousseau?" asked the elder Lord Westerfield.

"That is true. However, I have a trusted lady's maid who shall help me. She is quite superior in many ways to a relative."

"Then you are all set," declared the lord. "When is the wedding date?"

Anne decided that Lord Westerfield had not told his father much about the miserable affair regarding her brother. So she answered simply, "Soon. Perhaps in the early fall. We have not yet set a date."

"That is a good plan. Yes, a wedding in the fall. There will still be roses for the church."

They finished their tea and Anne declared that it was time for her to collect Jeremy and go home. He was summoned and, with his puppy in arms, properly thanked the elder lord for the visit and young Lord Westerfield for the gift of the puppy.

Then, Lord Westerfield held Anne's hand as they headed for the carriage. "May I see you tomorrow? I could come late in the afternoon. Father hates to dine alone, so I shall return before supper."

"That would be wonderful. Your father may soon have more company than he bargained for. He is not used to an active young boy at his table. And though I try to impress manners upon Jeremy, he forgets himself upon occasion."

He gave her fingers a gentle squeeze. "I assure you that he will enjoy it. As he said himself, it stirs him up to have Jeremy's young company. I predict that they will be the best of friends."

She smiled. "I am sure you are right."

He helped her into the carriage and slowly released her hand. It seemed harder to let her go each time they parted. He consoled himself with the thought that they would soon be man and wife and would no longer live apart. Then, they might see each other every day whenever they liked.

Anne watched the puppy squirm as they rode along and thought of how much the little creature reminded her of Jeremy when he was young. He was always squirming to get down and be about his own business. She could not help but smile. Duke had the makings of an agreeable pet, and with Lord Westerfield to help raise him, they were sure to have a fine dog one day.

They arrived home and Anne went straight away to ask after Mr. Tyler. She had not seen him all day yesterday and wondered how he was faring since the disturbing letter arrived. She hoped the strain had not been bad for his health.

She was unable to find out since Polly told her that Mr. Tyler had gone to ride about the estate earlier in the morning and had not returned. Anne sighed as she hung her bonnet beside the door. Perhaps the fresh air would do him good. Yet, it was growing quite warm and she wished he would return. If he did not return soon, she feared he would become overheated and do himself harm.

Before she could think about it any further, she heard Polly answer the door. She stepped into the library where Anne was choosing a book to say, "Mrs. Fletcher to see you, miss."

Anne felt her mouth drop in surprise. The last person she expected to call upon her was Mariah Fletcher. She instructed Polly to show her in and steeled herself to face whatever complaint Mariah might have against her.

When Mariah entered, Anne noticed straight away that her friend had grown pale. She looked no happier than she had last evening at the ball. Still wondering about the purpose of the visit, she invited Mariah to sit.

She sat stiffly in the straight-backed chair. Anne noticed that the tiny mint flowers on her dress nearly matched the leaves on the fabric of the chair. They sat, unspeaking and uncomfortable in one another's presence. Anne rubbed her slippers in the rich swirl of the Persian rug and said, "Might I get you anything? A cup of tea, perhaps?"

Mariah caught her lip between her teeth. "No thank you. I do not require anything. Not anything except a friend, at least."

To Anne's surprise, Mariah drew out a lacey white kerchief and began to dab at the tears that coursed down her cheeks. Anne felt too stunned to do anything except stare. She had hoped for their reconciliation and expected chastisement. She had not expected tears.

Finally, she sat forward in her chair and touched Mariah's arm. "Mariah, dear, whatever is the matter?"

"You must think me quite the fool. You were right and I was wrong."

Anne frowned, truly unable to follow her train of reasoning.

"Whatever do you mean? I have not thought anything of the kind."

"Well, you should have. I would deserve it."

Mariah wiped at the tears that stained her cheeks. Her red-rimmed eyes and sagging shoulders attested to the depth of her distress. She pulled a deep breath and said, "Surely you could never forgive me for the way I have cut you. It was not entirely my idea. Mr. Fletcher suggested it. I believe he was angry because you had refused him."

"I see."

"And last night when I saw you with Lord Westerfield I knew that there was something between you. I could tell by the way he looked at you. It is true, is it not?"

Anne felt at a disadvantage admitting her engagement until she knew what Mariah was going to say. Instead of replying, she asked, "Have we caused your current distress?"

Mariah shook her head. "La, you are in no way responsible for the fix I find myself in. If I were smart like you, I would not find myself in such a position at all."

As Mariah looked likely to burst into fresh tears, Anne hurried to say, "I do not understand. What position are you in?"

"I am embarrassed to say, though I must confide in someone. I cannot tell Mama and Papa, not when they disapproved of the elopement. With them, I must go along and pretend that all is very well. But, as I said, I must tell someone. And you have always been my very best friend. I know I can trust you, though you must promise not to breathe a word that is said."

Anne nodded. "Only tell me what is troubling you so."

"It is Mr. Fletcher."

"Mr. Fletcher?"

"Yes. It seems he never truly intended to buy a home. He is destitute from his debts. He was becoming desperate to marry, for he had no more money for the inn. He would marry or be thrown out on the street."

Anne's breath caught in her throat, making her speechless. While she had not thought Mr. Fletcher a suitable match for herself, she had never imagined that he was no more than a finely wrapped package. How could she console Mariah for becoming prey to such a scoundrel?

Yet, determined to try, she said, "Perhaps he admitted all of this because he loves you and wants to be honest with you."

Mariah shook her head, causing her shiny blond curls to bob. "He does not love me. He as good as said so. He laughed at me and said I am as witless and empty-headed as a pheasant and twice as easy to catch. Oh, Anne, what a foolish girl I have been to allow him to appeal to my vanity, and then, be annoyed by your warning. I should have listened to you."

"You could not have known."

"Yes, but what can I do? I cannot throw him out. Think of the embarrassment it would cause to me and my family. And I cannot go away with him. We have no money. And I would rather die than ask Papa to fund us any."

"No. It is no good to go away. I doubt he is suited for any work that would acceptably support you. You must remain here for now. Tell your Papa that Mr. Fletcher's investments have gone badly and that he is down in his fortunes. Surely, he will let you stay on."

"For now, perhaps. But what about when Papa dies? My cousin, Thomas, will inherit and will surely want us to vacate. What will we do then?"

Anne patted her hand. "Try not to worry. Perhaps by then, Mr. Fletcher will inherit property of his own. Has he not a father in London?"

"I do not know. He will not tell me."

"You must ask about his prospects. Perhaps all as not as ill as you fear."

Mariah wiped her eyes. "Dear Anne. You always make me feel better just by talking to you. Will you forgive me for cutting you so? I will not do it again, no matter what Mr. Fletcher says."

"Of course I forgive you. And I have a secret for you."

Anne's eyes shone as she leaned forward and said, "Lord Westerfield and I are to be married."

Mariah clasped Anne's hands. "I knew it. I am so happy for you. He has a fine estate and you will not have to worry about money."

Anne laughed. "La, I am not marrying him for his money."

Mariah sighed. "I know that. Yet, it is important, you know."

"I suppose you are right."

"Think about it. You will be the mistress of an estate. And to think that I had the nerve to strut like a peacock and look down upon you. Me, the wife of a penniless rogue."

Anne gave Mariah's fingers a gentle squeeze. "Now that we are good friends again we shall not think of that anymore. We shall put it all behind us."

"Where shall the wedding be?"

"In the village church, with a banquet to follow. But first, there shall be a small party to announce the event. The elder Lord Westerfield insists upon it."

"Oh, I do hope Mr. Fletcher will agree that we should go."

"You must, for it would not be half so much fun without you."

Mariah's eyes sparkled. "This will make up for my silly impulse to run off and get married. I cannot wait. When shall it be?"

Anne puckered her brow. "I do not know exactly."

She relayed the story of what had happened with Jeremy and Lord Tyler's son.

"Why that is dreadful," Mariah said. "You must be mad with worry."

"We are keeping a close watch on Jeremy. It is hard for him not to be able to run freely about."

"Yes, but you dare not let him until the ugly business is settled. You say you have no recognition of the man?"

"No. I have never seen him. But the note sent to Mr. Tyler was posted at the village."

"That is frightening, indeed. I wonder why no one has noticed a stranger about."

"Perhaps he is posing as a tenant or other worker. Mr. Tyler thought he might be our new groom, but he was not."

"This is frightful. If there is anything that I can do, you will let me know, will you not?"

"Indeed. We sent him over to Lord Westerfield last night for safekeeping."

"I should be glad to watch over him too if the need arises."

"I know you would."

After a few more moments of chat, Mariah said that she must leave. "I told Mr. Fletcher that I was going on a buggy ride. If I am away too long, he will question me. That is another thing that I do not like. He is always questioning me."

"Perhaps you may learn to overlook it."

Mariah pursed her lips. "I hope so."

She looked forlorn as she bid Anne good-bye and settled into the buggy. Anne watched her ride away and thought that such a marriage must be quite a trial. And to think that she had once been Mr. Fletcher's object of prey. He had tried all the same lies on her and failed.

She shivered. But what if she had succumbed to them?

She was comforted by the fact that Lord Westerfield was not marrying her for her money. Of that, she was sure. With bountiful lands, tenants, and a grand old estate, he would never want for funds.

She questioned her heart as to whether any of these things had determined her decision to marry him and decided they had not. Only love and love alone would ever have induced her to marriage. And she loved Lord Westerfield with all of her heart. Of that she was sure.

She lunched with Jeremy who complained at having to leave the puppy tied outside the kitchen while he dined. "He gets lonely all by himself."

"He will be fine. He must get used to being alone sometimes. Cook will not like having a puppy underfoot if you leave him in the kitchen."

Jeremy grinned. "I took him out to the garden while you were talking to Mrs. Fletcher. He had such fun chasing a butterfly. You should have seen him. His floppy ears were bouncing and he tripped over his long puppy legs."

Anne frowned. "Did you forget that you are not supposed to leave the house? Have one of the servants take the puppy out for his walks in the garden."

"I stayed near the house and I did not see anyone at all. I am so tired of staying inside."

"Nonetheless, you must promise that you will not go out with the puppy. If you do not promise, I shall take Duke straight back to Lord Westerfield."

Jeremy sat straight up in his chair. "Do not do that. Oh, please, Anne. I will not go out with him again."

She smiled. "I believe you. But remember our bargain."

"I will."

After lunch, they went to their chambers for an afternoon rest.

Anne stared out her window to see dark clouds roiling and billowing. It would surely rain. And very soon. It would break the morning heat that had felt sticky and oppressive. She longed to roost with a cozy book while she drifted to sleep.

Yet, she stood frowning and wondering what had become of Mr. Tyler. Surely he could see the upcoming storm. He would be caught in it if he did not return soon.

She pushed her worries aside. He was a sensible man. Perhaps he had gone to the village and would sit out the storm safely in a pub.

More than likely that was the case and she was silly to stand here watching the sky and fretting.

She settled comfortably in her bed and opened her book. After a while, the words began to blur. She set the book beside her and drifted into a cozy nap.

She was awakened sometime later by fierce thunder that shook the windows and rattled the ground. She sat up and stared at the rivulets pouring down the window. She forced herself to budge from her cozy nest and plod to the window to see the brilliant streaks of lightning that filled the gray sky. From the look of the storm, it seemed they were in for a drenching.

She wondered if Mr. Tyler had returned.

She was just turning her doorknob to check on his whereabouts when a knock sounded at the door. She opened the door to see Polly standing outside. The girl was as white as her starched bib and she was shaking like a leaf.

"Please, miss, you had better come down."

CHAPTER ELEVEN

ANNE FOLLOWED POLLY down the stairs.

"Whatever is the matter?"

Between sobs, Polly said, "It is Mr. Tyler, miss."

"Where is he?"

"In the kitchen."

At the bottom of the stairs, Anne brushed past the girl and hurried to the kitchen. She supposed he must have been caught in the storm after all. Perhaps he had been thrown by his horse and knocked unconscious. He might have lain in a puddle for hours.

She entered the kitchen, prepared to suggest warm drinks and bundling off to bed. Betsy stopped her at the door. "You must prepare yourself, miss. It is not a pretty sight. Perhaps you should sit down first."

Anne peered past Betsy's sturdy shoulder to see Mr. Tyler laid out on the floor.

"I do not want to sit. I want to know what is wrong with him. Was he caught in the storm?"

"Not exactly, miss. He was shot."

"Shot?"

Understanding did not immediately register in Anne's mind. How could he be shot? He had gone riding across the fields, had he not? He was nowhere near the forest.

She edged past Betsy to see the young groom kneeling beside Mr. Tyler.

Her hand threw to her throat as she saw the large splotch of blood that stained the white rags they had applied to the wound in his chest.

"We have tried to get the bleeding stopped. But he has lost a great deal of blood," Betsy said.

"Have you sent for the doctor?"

Betsy nodded. "The 'ostler went right away."

Anne knelt beside him. "Mr. Tyler, can you hear me?"

His eyelids flickered but did not open. He was deathly pale.

"They sent me out looking when he did not return this afternoon," said Pete. "I found him lying wounded at the edge of the meadow."

"We should get him upstairs," Anne said.

Pete nodded.

As gently as could be managed, Pete and the butler carried Mr. Tyler up the stairs. When they had settled him in bed, Anne pulled up a chair and sat beside him. According to Pete and Betsy, the bullet had gone through his chest and out under his shoulder blade. No one knew exactly how long he had lain on the ground before he was found.

She watched the stain spread beneath the bandage and knew it was a grievous wound. His breathing was ragged and strained. Bubbles formed at his lips. The bullet had pierced his lung. She glanced at the clock and hoped the doctor could arrive in time to save him.

The rain continued to pour, blocking the view of the trees, as though a gray curtain had been pulled about the house, shutting them off from the world and isolating them to bear their calamities alone. Would there ever be a time when she would not live with the constant fear of losing those she loved? Her spirits sank into doldrums that matched the relentless rain.

After a while, he moved restlessly and opened his eyes. He reached weakly for her hand and said, "I do not believe he is my son. A son could not do this to his father, do you think?"

"Your son shot you?"

He nodded. "It must have been. Remember the note. He threatened to make me sorry for not getting the boy out of his way. He is a cold man. Cold and cruel. He takes pity on no one. Jeremy is in great danger since he stands between the inheritance. The man will come for him again now."

Anne's blood turned to ice. A man who was capable of murdering once would not hesitate to try it again. She must think of a way to protect Jeremy, find a place where he would be safe.

Mr. Tyler slipped back into unconsciousness, his breathing shallow and labored, then so quiet that she could not tell if he was breathing at all. She had just clasped his wrist, trying desperately to feel his pulse, when the doctor bustled into the room.

Anne stepped aside to let him examine the patient.

After a moment, he stepped back, solemnly shaking his mop of white hair. "Maybe if I had got to him sooner. Yet with such a critical wound, there was probably little I could have done."

"He is gone?"

The doctor nodded.

Tears welled in Anne's eyes. She had known Mr. Tyler for a very short time. Yet, in that time, she had become fond of the kindly gentleman and sorry for the circumstances that had almost laid waste to his life.

She looked up to see Jeremy standing in the doorway. His blue eyes were wide with curiosity. "What is wrong with Mr. Tyler? Why is he sleeping so late in the day?"

Anne rushed out to him, closing the door behind her. She glanced up at Betsy and Polly who were gathered in the hall.

"Send word to Lord Westerfield that he is wanted as soon as he might arrive. And send to the village and inform the parson and magistrate of what has happened."

Betsy nodded her graying head and said, "Then Mr. Tyler....he is...?

"Yes. Jeremy and I shall go and talk. You may show the doctor out when he is ready to leave."

"Yes, miss."

Polly began to sob and Betsy sent her downstairs.

Anne led Jeremy toward his room.

"Why is everyone so sad?" he asked.

"Come in and I shall tell you."

Jeremy settled onto the floor and pulled the sleepy puppy onto his lap. He began to stroke the silky ears as he waited for Anne to explain. She hesitated, hating to break the news, yet knowing she must.

"You know that we have been worried that Mr. Tyler's son might pull a mischief?"

"I remember. That is why I have not been permitted to leave the house."

"Yes. Well, he is angry with his father, also. Today when Mr. Tyler went out riding, someone shot him. He believed it may have been his son."

Jeremy's hand froze mid-stroke and he stared solemnly at Anne. "Is he going to be alright?"

Anne blinked back a tear that threatened to slip down her cheek. "No, dear. He was too badly wounded. He died just a little while ago."

"And I did not get to tell him good-bye? It is not fair. Grandfather is gone and now Mr. Tyler."

After his burst of anger, he slumped over the puppy and began to cry. The little creature whined and licked his face. Anne put her arms around both of them.

"I am so sorry. I know you liked him very well and so did I. But we must think of you now and how to keep you safe. Mr. Tyler's last words were about you."

Jeremy looked up with pools of liquid in his blue eyes. "He thinks I am next, does he not, that I will die, too?"

"No. He only wanted me to keep you safe."

"How will we do that?"

"I do not know. But we will find a way. I have asked Lord Westerfield to come over. Perhaps he can help us."

She left Jeremy to mourn while she walked downstairs to lock all the windows and doors and inform the staff to be alert. Betsy had already begun preparing Mr. Tyler for burial. Anne knew that it would fall to her to arrange the ceremony.

Anne and Jeremy ate little supper and spoke even less. They were tense. The obvious absence of Mr. Tyler made them conscious both of their loss and of the peril that lay beyond their walls.

After supper, Anne paced the house waiting for Lord Westerfield, who did not arrive until quite late.

She met him in the entrance hall. He took her hands in his own and said, "I came as soon as I could. I was detained by the storm far out on one of my tenant's land. I did not get home until a little while ago."

Her knees felt weak from forcing herself to carry on all day. Now, as the loss and strain caught up with her, she wilted into him, grateful for the support of his strong arms.

He led her gently to the parlor and saw her safely settled on the settee. In a tone of utmost concern, he said, "Are you ill? Is there something I may get for you? The doctor, perhaps?"

"No. The doctor has already been here today, but not for me."

She buried her face in her hands and said, "It is too terrible. I do not know what we shall do."

He knelt beside her and took her hands. "Pray tell me what has happened."

Anne relayed all that she knew about the attack on Mr. Tyler. When she finished, she noticed by the clench of his jaw and the intensity of his gaze that Lord Westerfield shared her anger and fear. Yet what could they do?

He clenched his fist and said, "One thing for sure. The boy cannot keep hiding in the house all his life."

Anne stared at him in shock. "You would have me send him out, no matter the risk."

He looked chagrined. "Of course not. I only meant that we must find a way to flush out the murderer."

"How?"

"We must make him believe that Jeremy is unguarded and may be caught alone."

"But we do not even know who the murderer is."

"That is why we must force him into the open."

"I will not allow Jeremy to be put at risk."

"Nor would I. But we know that Mr. Tyler's son watches the grounds. Otherwise, he could not have shot his father. We will make a dummy in the height of a child and take him riding with me. If we are lucky, the fake Jeremy will be shot."

Anne nodded as understanding dawned upon her. "Then Tyler will feel it safe to come forward and claim the estate. After all, we cannot prove anything against him."

"Exactly right."

Anne brightened. "It is worth a try. I shall start on it first thing in the morning."

"And I shall return for a ride."

Westerfield kissed her tenderly and made her promise to get some rest.

She locked up after him and went up to check on Jeremy. She found him wide-awake with his puppy lying on the end of his bed.

"You have not gone to sleep yet?"

"I am afraid of being murdered if I sleep. Maybe I should sleep on the secret stairs that lead behind Grandfather's room."

Anne shivered. "I do not think that having you die of consumption would be a better way to solve this problem."

She ruffled his hair. "Besides, a dormouse might bite you on the toe."

Jeremy shook his head. "Not if I had Duke with me."

"I do not think Duke would be happy on the dark stairs, either. You try to get some sleep. Lord Westerfield has come up with a plan for tomorrow."

Jeremy was intrigued by the idea of a dummy just like him and quickly offered to help with the stuffing. Anne was glad it gave him something to take his mind from the danger. By the time she left his room, his eyelids were closing in sleep.

She trod to her chambers and tried to rest. She dozed a bit and woke often, always listening for footsteps in the hall. Yet, she heard nothing but the whistling wind that blew incessantly throughout the night.

In the morning, both the vicar and the constable arrived. Anne arranged a graveside service to be held in the church cemetery in two days. Later, she endured questions from the constable, who insisted upon interviewing everyone who had known Mr. Tyler, especially Pete, who had been the one to find him. Though he seemed especially suspicious of the boy, he found nothing of use when he finished his inquiry. They were no nearer to solving the crime than when he had begun.

He promised to keep in touch and work toward locating young Mr. Tyler. Yet, with nothing to go on and no way to prove he was responsible for the crime, she feared the constable would soon grow weary with the case.

While Anne was busy, Betsy and Polly began to sew and stuff the dummy. Jeremy brought his hat and his brightest clothes and fastened them carefully in place. When they were done, even Betsy, who was an excellent seamstress, declared it a good likeness."

Lord Westerfield arrived. He looked at their creation and down at Jeremy. "A perfect likeness, my boy, with a head filled with fluff."

Jeremy grinned up at him. "My head is not filled with fluff."

Lord Westerfield ruffled his hair. "Indeed it is not."

Anne caught the lord's arm. "Now that we are ready, I am not so sure this is a good idea. What if you are shot?"

"There is no reason to shoot me. He has nothing to gain. He has already proved that he is an excellent shot. If we are lucky, he will take the bait. Now, go about your business and keep Jeremy out of sight."

Jeremy thought it the greatest excitement. He paced and chattered and speculated upon when he would be shot. Anne felt her nerves strung tight and tried several times to get him to hush. She was unsuccessful until the arrival of their company caused her to send him to the kitchen to pester Cook.

"Mr. and Mrs. Fletcher, miss. I have shown them into the parlor," said Polly.

Anne felt in no frame of mind to endure the stream of neighbors who would begin drifting by to extend their sympathy. Yet, Mariah was her friend and welcome comfort even if she was accompanied by Troy.

She found them standing in the parlor engaged in conversation. From their stiff stance and red faces, she inferred that she had interrupted a disagreement. From what Mariah had told her, she assumed they endured a great many disputes.

Mariah rushed forward. "We just heard about poor Mr. Tyler. How did it happen? Was it a hunting accident?"

"I do not believe so. We think it was a deliberate act of murder."

Mariah's eyes grew wide. "You told me about the danger, yet I can hardly believe such a thing could happen. Surely it is too horrible to be true."

"If I am to keep Jeremy safe, I must believe it."

Troy shook his head. "Surely you cannot believe that someone intends to harm the boy."

"I have every reason to believe it."

He frowned. "Then why do you not send him away. Surely it would be safer than keeping him here."

"Mr. Tyler thought so, too. But I do not believe it to be the best course. If he were discovered, there would be no one to look out for him."

Mariah nodded. "That is true, the poor dear."

Anne invited them to sit. Mariah then explained briefly to her husband the story behind the inheritance. When she concluded, he frowned and said, "Why do you assume it is the son who has killed Mr. Tyler? Surely he might have other enemies."

"That is true," Anne agreed. "But they would have nothing to gain from his death."

Troy rubbed his chin and Anne noticed that he now sported a fashionable goatee. He studied her a moment as though mulling over the information and said, "No, I do not believe it that it is the son. It would be too obvious when he came to inherit. Do you not think it more likely that someone was blackmailing Mr. Tyler? Perhaps he was killed when he refused to pay."

Anne frowned. She had never thought of such a possibility. She wanted to believe it, because, then, Jeremy would be out of danger. And yet, the facts did not fit.

She shook her head. "What about the tutor? Polly told us that when he was killed, she overhead a threat against my brother."

Troy laughed abruptly. "Polly is an imbecile of a girl. I would not believe all that she says."

Mariah shot him a disapproving glare. "I am sure Anne does not need to hear us criticize her choice of maids."

He sat back and rubbed his chin. "I am sorry. I shall stop intruding now and behave myself."

True to his word, he listened to the women and did not say another word until the end of the visit. Then he saluted smartly to the small figure in the doorway. Anne glanced up to see Jeremy framed there.

Troy looked the boy up and down and said, "He looks healthy enough."

"And he shall stay that way," Anne retorted.

"Indeed, you are doing all that you can," Mariah assured her. "It is time that we left or we shall surely wear you out."

As she saw her guests to the door, Anne wondered how Lord Westerfield had fared. It was two more hours before he returned, tired and hot with no sign of the killer.

They withdrew to the drawing-room to speak. Westerfield studied her worried face and said, "I am afraid it did not work this time, though I do not think we should give up. Perhaps I shall try again tomorrow."

"The funeral for Lord Tyler is tomorrow. What shall I do with Jeremy? I dare not let him go and I do not want to leave him here with only the servants."

"We will take him back to my father. I can post some of the groomsmen to keep guard. Furthermore, no one will know he is there."

Anne nodded. "That would ease my mind since it would be a bit awkward if I did not attend the funeral."

"We shall both attend. But, first, we will drop Jeremy at Westerfield Manor."

She looked deeply into his dark eyes. "I do not know what I would do without you."

"You shall not have to try. I intend to share both your joys and troubles for the rest of your life."

He cupped her chin and leaned down to claim her lips in a gentle kiss. Anne savored the warmth of his mouth, the familiar scent of his cologne. He was like a safe oasis in a desert. She longed to cling to him and forget about the danger that lurked like a dark and unknown shadow. She knew as soon as he left, her sense of safety would evaporate and the fearful feelings would return.

Moments later, he told her good-bye. He had to get back to his father and the account ledger that awaited his attention. All would be well, he assured her.

"Keep your courage, my dearest. I will be back in the morning."

She bid him good-bye and then turned with a frown at the tumult emanating from the hall. She made straight for Jeremy to tell him he must keep the puppy quiet in the house when she saw the source of excitement.

Jeremy dragged the dummy along the floor while the puppy pounced and barked and nipped at it with his sharp little teeth. Jeremy grinned in glee. When he saw Anne, he looked up and said, "See how he loves this game? It is better than tugging on a rope."

Anne stooped to pick up the puppy, which was quite an armful by now. He wriggled and squirmed and tried to return to the game. "Stop that at once. We may need that dummy again. Anyway, you do not want to teach the puppy to attack. He is a hunting dog, remember?"

Jeremy jutted his chin. "Why is it when I am having fun I must always stop? You are often cross with me now."

Anne handed him the puppy. "I am sorry. How would you like to go and visit at Westerfield Manor again tomorrow?"

Jeremy brightened. "I should like that. Lord Westerfield plays games with me. And he tells me all sorts of stories. He has been many places you know. He was even in India once."

Anne smiled at him. "Then you must have a great deal to talk about. Lord Westerfield and I shall drop you there in the morning before we go to the service for Mr. Tyler."

She handed Jeremy the silky, wriggling pup. "Take him upstairs, will you dear, and play with him in your room. I must take care of overseeing flowers for the church and gravesite.

Anne spent the rest of the day making sure the details of the funeral were in order. The undertaker came for the body and all was set for the service in the morning. She still could not believe Mr. Tyler had passed so rapidly through their lives. Sometimes it seemed as though it all must be a dream. Yet, when she awakened the next morning, nothing had changed.

The chill in her room made her wonder if it was going to be a damp day. She trod to the window and surveyed the overcast sky. In the distance, poplars swayed in the brisk breeze like a row of dancers.

Anne shivered, dreading the dismal melancholy of burying poor Mr. Tyler during a drizzle. Yet, after the tragic events of his life, perhaps it was fitting that it be a rainy day when he was buried.

Such cheerless thoughts brought tears to her eyes. She determined to shake herself from her gloom and rouse Jeremy. He must prepare for his trip to Westerfield Manor if they were going to leave within the next hour.

She prodded Jeremy into getting dressed and summoned Pete to take Duke on his morning walk. Jeremy gave his hair a disinterested swipe and asked, "May I bring Duke? I do not want him to be lonely."

Anne picked up the brush and carefully groomed his wavy dark locks while he grimaced and tried to dodge out of her reach.

"I do not think you had better bring him. It would not be polite to do so without an invitation. We can tie him outside the kitchen where he can watch Cook at her work."

Satisfied with her job, Anne replaced the brush upon the dresser. "It is only for part of the day. He will be fine."

They breakfasted on sticky buns, melon balls, and ripe berries. Then they settled in the drawing-room to wait upon Lord Westerfield.

He was not long in coming. He appeared at the stroke of nine and greeted them cheerily. "How are my two favorite Tylers? I trust you both slept well."

Jeremy shook his head. "Duke woke me in the middle of the night. He needed to go out and poor Pete had to take him. I wish Duke could use a chamber pot."

Anne felt her cheeks grow hot with mortification. She turned to him and said, "Jeremy, of all the things to say! Surely you must know better."

Her chastisement would have been more effective had not Lord Westerfield collapsed into a fit of mirth, laughing so hard that he bent double and put his hand upon the chair for support. Jeremy grinned broadly as though he had made a fine joke and Anne, being out-numbered gave up her attempt at a reprimand. She was, at least, comforted by the fact that they got on so well together.

Anne collected her shawl and black crinoline bonnet that she had worn at Grandfather's funeral. She felt dowdy in the black crepe dress and hoped that she would have no further reason to wear it.

They boarded the carriage just as the sky released the moisture it had been holding. The rain splashed in fat drops that plopped upon the ground and the roof of the carriage.

They left Jeremy off with Lord Westerfield, who was more than pleased with his company. Anne wished secretly that she might have stayed also. She had no desire to endure the sadness of the kind gentleman's funeral. Yet with her own Lord Westerfield by her side, she would manage satisfactorily. She only hoped the rain would stop before they all trod out to the gravesite.

CHAPTER TWELVE

.. ❧ ..

ANNE NOTICED THAT THE mourners were nearly all single women, two dozen, at least. The rain had let off and they milled about chatting and exchanging news. Presently the whole assembly entered the church where the ladies set cakes and punch on the table in the foyer.

Amidst the expressions of sympathy sent her direction, Anne overhead more than one comment to the effect of, "We met in the apothecary one day. He was such a nice man and a widower, too."

"He always spoke to me. We were particular friends."

She sighed. Mr. Tyler had been an eligible bachelor and a good catch. No wonder there were so many disappointed souls assembled at the church. She wondered how many had pressed attention upon him during his trips to the village.

She was happy to see Mariah when she arrived, flanked by Troy, who looked less than happy to be there. Mariah leaned from the pew behind them to whisper, "It looks as though Mr. Tyler was popular with the ladies."

Despite herself, Anne could not suppress a smile. "It is interesting how he never mentioned one of them."

"You believe the affection was one-sided."

"Yes. I believe that it was."

They settled back quietly as the service began. After a few hymns, the vicar delivered the eulogy and then the prayer. When he had finished, he invited the congregation to follow the coffin to the gravesite beside the church.

Anne clutched Lord Westerfield's arm as they followed the men who bore the casket. She was aware of the unabashed stares from the ladies of the church. The gossip would fly until they learned of the engagement. Then each would be quick to assure the others that she was the first to deduce there had been an attachment.

At the gravesite, the vicar read scripture as the casket was lowered. Anne listened, fighting back tears when he finished. Everyone watched as she tossed a handful of dirt upon the casket. The service ended and people began to drift away, drawn by the refreshments waiting in the parlor. At last, only Mariah and Troy were left with Anne and Lord Westerfield.

Mariah touched Anne's elbow. "I am so sorry. You have had many losses to bear."

Anne nodded. "I did not know him long and yet, I found him kind and understanding. Both Jeremy and I shall miss him."

She smiled at Mariah. "Thank you for coming. And you, too, Mr. Fletcher."

Mariah pressed her lips into a disapproving line. "We nearly missed it entirely. Mr. Fletcher has taken to going out for a hunt each morning, though I do not know why as he is yet to come back with any game. He went out today and only just remembered in time that we had an engagement."

A glance at Troy told Anne that he did not appreciate Mariah's assessment of his activities. The smoldering resentment that lay in his eyes made her shiver and feel glad that she had not become mixed up with him.

In a cold tone, he replied, "Thank you for sharing my lack of ability, my dear. Perhaps I might do the same for you sometime."

Mariah's rosy cheeks flushed bright crimson.

"Forgive me," she said stiffly. "I did not mean to offend."

"Perhaps we should all go in for some refreshment. It has turned quite warm after the rain," said Lord Westerfield.

Anne quickly agreed. She welcomed a diversion to relieve the tension. "Yes, we must. I am sure the ladies would be offended if we did not partake."

They sampled cake and punch and drifted about the room chatting with the ladies. The widow Needleham surprised Anne by saying, "I was delighted to hear of your engagement, dear. Mariah told me about it when we spoke a few minutes ago. I should be glad to help with preparations in any way that I can."

Anne managed a smile. "Thank you. You are very kind to offer."

The lady leaned toward Anne and whispered conspiratorially, "I was surprised by Mariah's elopement. If you ask me, it was all very strange."

Anne decided to change the subject. "Indeed. Now I would like to ask you if we shall be able to count on you for roses should I fall short. You have such beautiful roses."

Mrs. Needleham beamed. "Oh, indeed. Of course, you may count on my roses. I should be delighted to share them."

They spoke of the flowers until the good lady decided it was time for her to take leave. "I need to get off these feet. I tire more quickly these days."

Anne smiled. "Then you must go home for a rest."

After Mrs. Needleham departed, Anne sought out Mariah for a private word. "Why did you tell Mrs. Needleham of the engagement? It was still a secret. Now everyone will know."

Mariah shrugged apologetically, "They would know soon enough anyway. Besides, you know how much I love to be the first to share any good news."

It was true. Anne knew that Mariah had never been able to bear keeping a happy secret. Though Anne had hoped to put off being a source of gossip for at least a few more days, she supposed she could easily forgive Mariah after what she had been through lately.

However, she did know that an upturn in social calls would be inevitable now. Being that she was a private person, and used to having her life to herself, they would surely tax her energy. Every matron in town would offer her advice in the choosing of her wedding clothes.

She looked up to see Lord Westerfield striding towards her, tall and fit, with just enough swagger in his step to convey confidence. He was worth any amount of having ladies meddle in her affairs.

As the guests departed, Anne thanked everyone for their kind condolences. When she closed the door, she felt as though she had used every reserve of energy she had ever possessed. Lord Westerfield led her to the couch, "Are you tired?"

"A little," she admitted.

He snuggled her against him. "You have a rest. You deserve it after what you have been through of late."

She rested her head against his shoulder and enjoyed the scent of his cologne and the slight stubble of his beard as it rubbed against her hair. She looked up, observing his chin and decided he was a man who must shave more than once a day.

He studied her upturned face. "What is so interesting?"

"You. I would memorize every detail of your face. You have a pirate's face, you know."

"A pirate's face?"

He sounded so surprised that she laughed.

"A very handsome pirate with black eyes and hair and a strong jaw."

He leaned down so close that his mouth was just above her own. "And how would you know anything about pirates?"

"I suppose I do not," she whispered, captivated by his closeness.

"Have you ever had a pirate do this?"

He kissed the top of her forehead.

She shook her head.

"Or this?"

He kissed her nose.

Once again, she shook her head.

"Or this?"

He captured her lips in a lingering kiss. She smelled of lilacs. He breathed in her scent as though he could store it in his lungs, to be reminded of her any time he liked.

He tasted of mint. Anne had often seen him, lost in thought as he chewed on a sprig. He had done so after their picnic. She would always remember him on that day, tall and handsome as he walked beside her.

They drew back and looked into one another's eyes.

He ran his fingers along her cheek, her temple, and the edge of her chin. "I know your lovely face, every line, and curve. I could pick you from a hundred women in a pitch-black cave."

Anne smiled. "You are a dear. You make me feel special."

He raised a brow. "You are special. I love you with all of my heart."

She snuggled against him again. "I love you, too. All the same, please stay out of dark caves full of women."

He laughed. "I think I can safely promise that I shall."

She sighed. "I suppose we should collect Jeremy from your father's care."

They had a carriage summoned and arrived at Westerfield Manor where Jeremy was in no hurry to be collected. "Lord Westerfield has given me leave to explore the house."

He barely stopped to explain before excusing himself for a further expedition. Therefore, Anne and the young lord were easily persuaded to stay and have a cup of afternoon tea with the elder Lord Westerfield.

"Nasty matter with Mr. Tyler. Jeremy told me all about it. What are you doing at home to see to the boy's protection?"

"I no longer allow him to play outside," Anne replied.

The aged man frowned. "And the servants? Do they look after him?"

"Yes, sir, my Betsy is careful to keep an eye on him."

He shook his head. "Poor boy. No one should have to live this way. Creeping about in shadows and hiding."

Just then Jeremy showed up. "I did not find any secret doors such as are in our house, Anne."

He said it with such somber disappointment that Anne smiled. "I do not suppose that every house has secret doors. However, I am sure you had a lovely time exploring."

He brightened. "Yes. It was glorious."

He spent several minutes telling of the glass case he had found full of carvings from India. The library was another of his favorite spots. With wide eyes, he related finding shelves of books that described all sorts of foreign lands.

"You must come and read them," said the young lord.

"I should be happy to. Any time," Jeremy returned politely.

Anne smiled at him. He was a winsome creature when his manners were intact.

When it was nearly time to leave, the elder lord said, "I should like to invite Miss Tyler and young Jeremy to a little party with some of the neighbors. Would Saturday night be convenient?"

Anne thought a moment. "It would be quite convenient."

He beamed. "Good. Then I shall begin planning."

Anne and Jeremy bid him good-day and set off for the trip home in the buggy with young Lord Westerfield. He gazed into Anne's eyes and said, "My father means to announce our engagement. I think he is still afraid you will get away."

Anne grinned at his candid assessment. "Tell him wild horses could not drag me away."

"I am glad of that."

When they arrived home, Jeremy jumped from the carriage to go and see his puppy. Anne sat with Lord Westerfield, neither wishing to part.

"Would you not like to come in?" she asked.

"I should get back soon. Now that Father has taken it into his head to have a party, he will want to begin preparations. And when he said he would begin planning, he meant that he would plan and I would carry it out."

"I see. Perhaps I could be of assistance."

He gave her an appraising look. "Perhaps you could. You could kiss a weary drudge to carry him through the ordeal of pleasing his father with the planning of a dinner."

She leaned to kiss his cheek and he turned his head, meeting her lips with his own. She laughed and drew back. "You are an incorrigible rogue."

"Your kisses are as intoxicating as a fine wine. I cannot help myself."

She paused and listened. "You shall have to, for I hear Jeremy and it sounds as though something is amiss."

They sprang from the carriage and followed the sound of his voice. He was frantically calling his dog, his voice growing panicked when there was no joyful bark in reply.

Anne found him in the garden. "What is the trouble?"

"Duke is gone, leash and all. He must have pulled free. I have to find him."

Anne glanced around, remembering how Mr. Tyler had been taken unaware. "You go inside. I will look for Duke."

"But he is my dog," Jeremy protested, on the verge of tears.

"And you are in danger every moment you are outside."

Lord Westerfield leaned down to the boy. "You go on in and ask Cook what she knows. I will stay and help your sister search. If Duke is anywhere near, we will find him."

Reluctantly, Jeremy obeyed.

"Do you suppose he ran back to your place?" Anne asked.

"I suppose it is possible. If we do not find him, I will go and have a look around.

They searched for over an hour, failing to find any sign of the dog in pastures or gardens. Exhausted, Anne said, "I know you must return home. Your father will want you. I will tell Jeremy we think the dog may have gone back to your manor. That will give him some comfort."

"I will let you know if I find him. The grooms can help search around the stables."

"Thank you. I know I do not have to tell you how much Duke means to Jeremy."

Westerfield nodded. "Try not to worry, darling. Dogs like to wander, but they usually turn up."

She sighed. "He has lost so much. Surely, he will not have to lose Duke, too."

He put his arm around her and gave her a gentle squeeze. "All will be well, you will see."

She watched him drive off, praying in her heart that Duke had gone back to the manor. It made perfect sense. He was born there and that was where Jeremy had gone. Perhaps, he was only tracking Jeremy. He would be returned safely once Lord Westerfield found him.

With that comforting thought firmly in mind, she went up to share her conviction with Jeremy. She found him moping about the library. He looked up when Anne came in.

Eyes brimming with tears, he said, "You did not find him, did you? Cook does not know where he is either."

"He will turn up. Lord Westerfield has gone to see if he might have gone searching for you at Westerfield Manor. Dogs sometimes return to where they were born, you know."

Jeremy brightened. "Do you think so?"

"I believe it is a good possibility."

"May we go, too, Anne? We could leave right away."

"Certainly not. Lord Westerfield will let us know if he finds Duke. I am sure he will bring him here straight away."

Jeremy sighed. "But it is so hard to wait."

"Yes, dear. But it is safest for you."

They waited all afternoon and all evening. Jeremy paced restlessly about the house, asking every little while if Anne thought Lord Westerfield would come.

At last, she could put off sending him to bed no longer.

"Perhaps they have decided to keep Duke overnight. I am sure we will hear from Lord Westerfield in the morning."

Jeremy went reluctantly to bed.

Anne retired much later, having asked Betsy to split a night shift of keeping watch over the house. When she finally got to bed she sunk rapidly into sleep and would have slept much later had not Jeremy knocked at her door at eight o'clock in the morning.

He popped inside and said, "Lord Westerfield has not come."

"It is too early for him to come. Please, Jeremy. Go and let me sleep."

He shut the door and trudged away. Though the house was quiet, Anne found that she could not get back to sleep. She tossed and turned and thumped her pillow into a dozen shapes. Still, each time she closed her eyes, all she could see was Jeremy's small face looking lonely and disappointed.

Finally, she gave up trying to rest and dressed for breakfast. She found Jeremy in the breakfast room, poking his fork at a poached egg and making no effort to eat it. Betsy looked up and said, "La, miss, you did not sleep long enough."

Anne stifled a yawn. "I slept as long as I could."

Betsy nodded at Jeremy. "I told the young master he needed to eat. He will not do that dog any good by losing his strength. I will tell Polly to fetch you some breakfast, too."

Anne settled at the table with Jeremy. "Betsy is right. You need to eat. When Duke returns, he will not want to find his master pale and sickly."

"What if he does not return? I shall never find a dog I like half so well."

"Do not think that way. You must not give up hope. Duke may yet be found."

After breakfast, she tried unsuccessfully to interest Jeremy in a geography game. They had been at it for only a short while when Polly announced that Lord Westerfield had arrived.

Anne sucked in her breath. Apprehension took away her usual delight in his arrival. So much was at stake. Jeremy would be so terribly disappointed if he did not have the puppy. And so blissfully happy if he did.

They hurried to the parlor where Lord Westerfield stood, quite alone.

Anne's heart sank. "You did not find Duke?"

He shook his head. "I was hoping he might have returned here."

"I am afraid he did not."

She bit her lip as she turned to Jeremy.

In an outburst of anger and pain, he cried, "I told you. He is gone and I shall not see him again."

Abruptly, he turned and spun from the room. A few moments later, they heard his footsteps pounding up the stairs.

"He is not taking it well," said Lord Westerfield. "He was very attached to the dog."

She nodded. "First he was not allowed out of the house for fear of his life and now his pet is gone. It has not been easy for him. And I do not know how to comfort him."

"There is very little you can do, except hope that Duke may yet return."

Anne shrugged. "I am afraid so."

"I have one more idea to try. If you have no objection, I shall ride out to your tenants and see if anyone has seen the dog. Perhaps someone took him in as a stray."

Anne's eyes filled with tears. "Truly you are kind to take such pains over Jeremy's loss. How can I thank you?"

He stepped over to her and pulled her to him. "You already thanked me by agreeing to become my wife. Your problems are my problems. Besides, I am quite fond of Jeremy. I know how it feels to love a pet so very dearly."

She smiled up at him, a dimple showing in her chin as she said, "I still say you are the dearest, kindest gentleman alive."

"And I say you are the sweetest, most beautiful creature on the face of the earth."

He kissed her softly, and then said, "I had better be off if I hope to visit all the tenants. With any luck, I shall find Duke with one of them."

"I do hope so."

She saw him out the door and then retreated to the massive oak desk in the library to look over their accounts. The tenants would owe them rent soon and Anne had never been the one responsible for collecting. As she flipped through the pages of figures, she wondered how Grandfather had ever kept it all straight. Though she showed more aptitude in mathematics than most girls she knew, with so many rows and columns, it would take quite a while to get it all straight.

She worked through the morning. Jeremy came in once and sat and read for a while. When she told him where Lord Westerfield had gone, he surprised her by saying, "I am sorry for shouting. I think it kind of you and Lord Westerfield to try so hard to find Duke."

Pride for him welled in her heart. She rose from the desk and knelt beside him. "You are a dear sweet boy. You have every right to worry over your pet."

His smooth brow wrinkled in determination as he said, "I shall try very hard to be brave."

She kissed his cheek. "I know you will, dear."

• • ❧ • •

THAT EVENING WHEN LORD Westerfield returned with unwelcome news, Anne knew that Jeremy would have to be very brave, indeed.

"One man with whom I spoke said he saw a fellow leave your lane carrying a pup away upon his horse. He described the dog as looking a great deal like Duke. He did not pay much attention to the man. He said he was dressed well and rode a fine bay."

"Oh dear, then Duke has been stolen?" Anne asked.

"It seems that way."

"But why would anyone do such a thing, especially a gentleman?"

Lord Westerfield shook his head. "That is a puzzle. Perhaps someone in town has seen the man or pup. I shall make a new inquiry tomorrow."

She clasped his fingers. "Thank you. Perhaps he is keeping the pup in town."

The muscle in Lord Westerfield's jaw tightened. "If he is, I shall see that Duke is returned."

A search the next day raised no sign of the dog. As the days passed, Jeremy kept his promise to be brave. He spoke little about finding the dog and Anne knew he was losing hope.

Saturday night arrived and it was time for the engagement party. Anne imagined that the elder lord was in quite a state of excitement about the event. He had kept his son hopping for the last day or two getting all in order. And now, Jeremy was to come along and they were all to have a merry time.

They arrived to greet the first guests. Mariah and Troy attended as well as a few neighbors and Westerfield's friends from the village.

Jeremy sipped lemonade while the adults had fine champagne to celebrate. By the time they sat to supper, Anne felt more festive than she had in many weeks. The sideboard was set with a bountiful feast of roast pheasant and hams, side dishes, puddings and cakes. She kept an eye on Jeremy who partook of so many sweets she was afraid he would suffer a stomach ache. Yet, she could not bring herself to chastise him. He had moped about, eating so little the last few days, that it was good to see him enjoy a meal.

When they finished, the gentlemen went to the drawing-room for a smoke while the ladies retired to the parlor. When Jeremy begged permission to go to the library, Anne agreed. He could amuse himself there until the evening ended.

Alone in the parlor, the ladies took pleasure in reminiscing about their weddings, all except Mariah. Anne's heart went out to her friend at her discomposure. However, when it came to advice and offers of assistance, the ladies all joined in, offering more than one conflicting opinion of what fashion would suit Anne best.

All the while Jeremy sat alone in the library, paging through Lord Westerfield's books. He was so engrossed in the geography about China that he hardly noticed when the door opened and a gentleman came in, holding a lantern in one hand.

"Jeremy, come with me. I know where to find your dog."

Jeremy jumped to his feet. "I shall tell Anne."

"No. Let us go alone and surprise her when we return with the puppy."

Jeremy thought that a splendid idea. After all, had not Anne and Lord Westerfield spent hours searching for Duke? Now, he could add to their happiness by surprising them with the puppy.

He followed along as the man said, "Let us go out the library door. No one will know we are missing until we return."

Moments later, Pete summoned Lord Westerfield as politely as he could manage. Alone in the hall, he stammered, "You told me to tell you if anyone came or went from the house. Master Jeremy just followed a fellow toward the forest."

Westerfield's heart began to pound. "Which way did they go?"

"Out the library, sir."

Westerfield strode to the library and took two loaded pistols from the desk. He stuck one behind his waistcoat and carried the other as he headed for the door.

Anne saw him pass the parlor and knew from the look on his face that something was amiss. She excused herself from the ladies and scurried to catch up with him. She called to him as he exited the open French doors.

"My lord, something is amiss. Please tell me what it is."

He glanced back. "No time to explain. I am going after Jeremy."

Anne's ire rose. Why would Jeremy wander from the house? He knew better than to worry them like this. He would catch the sharp edge of her tongue when they caught up with him.

She raised her skirts and dashed to keep Lord Westerfield in view as he ran toward the thicket of trees that bordered the gardens. Had it not been for the full moon, she knew she would have lost sight of him.

She was out of breath by the time he slowed at the edge of the trees. She caught up with him and grasped his arm as they plunged into the edge of the thicket.

"You should not have come. There may be danger. I only pray we are not too late." His grim words made her blood run cold.

"What do you mean?"

"Jeremy was not alone when he left the house."

They passed quietly among the trees, listening for any sound that would alert them to Jeremy's whereabouts. After a few moments, they heard a puppy's gleeful barking.

"Duke," Anne whispered.

They made their way straight for the sound of the puppy and stumbled into a small clearing. What they saw by the light of the lantern brought them to an abrupt halt. Anne felt faint with fright. Two large dogs, trapped in a pen, drew back their fangs and snarled at the new arrivals.

Her gaze flew from the dogs to the golden-haired man who stood a mere fifteen feet away, staring at them, his face distorted by the light at his feet. Startled by their sudden appearance, he grabbed Jeremy and held a knife to his throat.

"Let him go. I will pay twice as much as whoever has hired you," Anne cried.

His green eyes narrowed. "No one has hired me."

"But you are not a Tyler," she stammered.

"Am I not? I am Zachery Tyler, son of your esteemed Mr. Tyler." He spat the words.

"He refused to recognize me as his son, but he could not prove I was not. I took the name Fletcher and came to claim what should be mine. I had your grandfather poisoned, then my father shot in an "accident". Now it is this boy's turn to die. And I am afraid you will both have to die with him. It will be a tragedy that you three took a walk and fell prey to wild dogs."

Lord Westerfield held his gun level, still aimed at the madman.

Fletcher tightened his hold on Jeremy. "Throw your pistol on the ground or the boy dies now."

Westerfield paused, judging the distance. It would not be an easy shot in the poor lighting. He couldn't chance hitting Jeremy.

Fletcher shouted, "Now! I mean it." He pointed to the ground in front of them.

Westerfield tossed the gun on the ground.

Fletcher gestured with his head. "You two come and stand beside the pen."

As they moved to join Jeremy, he began to scream and kick at Fletcher. "No, I will not let you hurt Anne."

"Shut up!" Fletcher struggled to hold the boy.

Duke, upset by his master's struggle sprang at Fletcher and sunk his teeth into the arm that held the knife. With a cry of pain, Fletcher dropped Jeremy to struggle with the biting dog.

Anne grabbed Jeremy and pulled him away.

"I will kill you, you beastly mutt," Fletcher cried, aiming a kick at Duke. Duke avoided the kick and ran to Jeremy.

Acting fast, Westerfield pulled his second pistol out and aimed at Fletcher. "It is over Fletcher. Stand where you are," he shouted.

Fletcher stepped back. His mouth worked in surprise to see himself staring into the barrel of yet another pistol. He held up his hands. Hatred shone from his eyes as he saw there was no way he could win.

"You are coming back to face the charges of murder," Westerfield said.

Fletcher looked into the dog pen and back at his captors. "I think not, for I would surely be hung. My father was the death of my mother and he will be the death of me, too. But, like her, I shall choose how I will die."

He stared into the pen with the snarling dogs. He took a step toward them and Anne cried out. Once again, Duke sprang upon him, delaying him from leaping into the pen. Lord Westerfield dashed forward and cracked his pistol upon Fletcher's head. The man fell in a heap.

"We'll bind him and call for the constable."

Duke returned to Jeremy. "He was not a nice man. Good boy, Duke. You saved us."

Westerfield appraised Anne. "Jeremy looks to be holding up better than you. You are shaking badly. Do you need to rest before we start back?"

She shook her head.

As they walked back for ropes, Anne bit her lip. "Believe or not, I feel some sympathy for the poor tortured man and I feel terrible for Mariah. It will be a terrible stigma for her to have had a murdering husband."

Westerfield considered her sentiments. "It is sad for her, but Jeremy is safe now."

Jeremy looked up at them. His blue eyes glowed in the moonlight. "Who shall be my guardian?"

Westerfield put his arm around Anne's waist. "Why us, of course. Myself and my wife."

He smiled down at Anne, liking the sound of those words. She smiled back. Husband and wife, nothing could be more perfect.

She linked her arm across Jeremy's shoulders and Lord Westerfield's waist, as together, they walked back to the house.

When they arrived, Lord Westerfield sent a groom to get the constable. Then, he gathered a small party of men to bind Zachary Tyler and escort him to the stable to await the constable. Mariah would be spared embarrassment during the engagement festivity.

When the party ended, they broke the news to her. She wept while they escorted her safely to her parents' house. Anne could only hold her hand, sympathetic tears flowing freely along the way.

When she had been safely deposited, Lord Westerfield told Anne, "Now, I shall see you two safely home, though I doubt you are in any more danger."

"We owe you thanks for that," Anne declared, as she gazed at his handsome face lit by moonlight through the window of the coach.

"Are you really to be married?" Jeremy asked.

"Indeed we are," Anne answered.

"That is most excellent," Jeremy assured them.

"Your approval pleases me," Lord Westerfield assured him.

They rode into the moonlight with Jeremy sleeping on the seat and Anne snuggled against the shoulder of the man she loved. Soon they would be a family. The losses of her past were behind her and she looked forward to the future. THE END

I hope you enjoyed this novel. I would love your review.

For another Regency romance you may enjoy, CLICK HERE[1] to sign up and get the link.

ABOUT THE AUTHOR

A native of Houston, TX, Karen spent her early years enjoying life along the Gulf Coast. She attended Texas A&M as well as the University of Houston where she obtained a B.S. in early childhood education. She has written numerous articles and stories, books for children and novels for adults. She particularly enjoys writing contemporary and historical romance. She now lives in the Southwest with her family and assorted pets. To learn more, please visit https://kecogan.blog/ and https://www.facebook.com/karencoganfanpage/

Don't miss out!

Visit the website below and you can sign up to receive emails whenever Karen Cogan publishes a new book. There's no charge and no obligation.

https://books2read.com/r/B-A-QNTE-WHWO

BOOKS 2 READ

Connecting independent readers to independent writers.